DESIRES REBORN

PENNY PEPPER

Cover image ©Abigail Stevens
Cover design © Emma Sheehan
Author image © JJ Waller

Desires Reborn

Explicit Stories of Disability, Desire and Love

Revised 21st Anniversary Edition

by

Penny Pepper

Reviews

'A force of nature and a voice like no other. [Penny's work is] brilliantly funny, brilliantly frank…'
Liz Carr, Olivier award-winner, star of BBC's Silent Witness

'Penny Pepper's work is a virtuoso display of wit, invention and courage. It's thought provoking and funny and moving and makes us see the world differently.'
Dame Margaret Drabble

'A wonderful memoir, this is the great untold tale of our times told with passion, humour and a compellingly visceral energy. Penny Pepper's story is of a true struggle for liberation against the odds. Essential reading.'
Jake Arnott, best-selling British novelist author of The Long Firm (on First in the World Somewhere, 2017)

.

'This is a revolutionary book that will at once turn you on, change your thinking, make you laugh, cry and most of all realise that this kind of fiction is so long overdue it's almost criminal.'
Mat Fraser, actor, disabled activist (on Desires, 2003).

Desires Reborn is a great collection of stories. *Postcards for Jean* is worth the price of the book alone – a little masterpiece.
John O'Donoghue, poet and journalist and author of Sectioned: A Life Interrupted (Mind Book of the Year 2010)

To my friend Theresa, with love.

A rock, an angel and unsung hero of creative inclusion.

Thank you.

www.theresalydiacrafts.co.uk

Contents

Foreword

This edition of *Desires Returns: Explicit Stories of Disability, Desire and Love,* is in celebration of my short story collection, *Desires*, first published in softback 21 years ago when I won an Innovate Award run by Arts Council England.

These stories have stood the test of time, and I am proud of them. Official publication day was 20th March 2003. I was at BBC Broadcasting House with literary publicist Tony Cowell, brother of Simon Cowell. We were there to promote the book, with its bold cover art by acclaimed disabled artist Tanya Raabe Webber. However, those of you who know your history will remember 20th March 2003 as the day of the Invasion of Iraq. All but one of my interviews were cancelled and never rebooked. Great and dreadful history unravelled, and my fiery little book languished.

What has changed over the past 21 years? Are disabled people fully integrated and accepted in a three-dimensional sense, not only within society but within literature? No – sadly there is much more work to be done. Yet, disabled people have an extensive presence. Technology has evolved, which, some of the time, brings us a new democracy. And here I am, a mature writer, punky passion intact yet painfully conscious that we still control very little of our fictional narratives. The barriers against expressing the disability story within fiction remain. We are the last taboo within mainstream culture, and while the disability experience is, word-by-word, moving into the broader context of human experience, we are still up against it in our fight for stories that are written *by* us, not merely *about* us.

Concerning the broader depiction of disabled people in fiction – and in the case of this collection of erotica – mainstream society remains challenged by work that sets out to show disabled people within a true, three-dimensional dichotomy of relationships – the good, the bad, the lustful, and the virginal. My characters jostle alongside non-disabled people in a way I hoped and believed had never been done before – a true reflection of real life.

Since 2003, disabled people have been pilloried as fraudulent, hateful scroungers. Our exposure has risen without doubt, as we appear in everything from adverts to soap operas; celebrity dance shows to athletics – yet rarely in serious mainstream drama, and *very* rarely within literary or commercial fiction under our own terms.

As I said in 2003, we love, we lust, we crave. Technology has indeed given a means for us to share our stories between ourselves across different mediums, and yet for all its good, social media also breeds the hatred that governments have ignited. When can we break out of the imposed role of unworthy beggar, away from the pity pen or the care home in our unwelcome status as the passive, accepting cripple who should be grateful for what they get?

We do not have equity. They still write *about us, without us*, though there are some signs of improvement now that we have sensitivity reads, and disabled people within the creative sector are coming together to speak with a louder, unified voice.

I never gave up, in either my writing or my activism, and so here is *Desires Returns* – finally come of age, 21 years almost to the day since its first publication. The stories in this collection have kept their unexpected innocence despite their explicitness. I'm struck, too, by how sexual experience and sexual encounter unravel, whether it's the overheard liaison in *Postcards for Jean*, or the dark, lurid excesses in *Seven Days*. This reflected where we were in our fight for sexual freedoms at that time. A new, exclusive story, *Nippy Days*, provides another bawdy dollop of Penny Pepper sauce.

Desires Reborn comes to you now with love and a light-touch revision. Previously, it was sometimes categorised as 'sexy disability stories', but this is a label that limits their true intention. They express a delicate sense of yearning and new nervous lust. Every story *is* sexually explicit and uses humour, but they are also sombre and likely to remain challenging to some.

My journey as a writer since that time has taken me along many convoluted roads. I've found champions, gained readers and many opportunities, but there has been resistance. We still fight for our right to free sexual expression that doesn't categorise us as different, 'special', and never sexual. We remain the tragic, the triumphant, the superhuman, the scrounger. And to that we say, we are normal, we are human! Always here, in an awful and wonderful range of experience, desperation and joy.

Disabled people fall in love. Disabled people fuck. Disabled people break hearts and have hearts broken. Disabled people fail and flourish. Disabled people marry and have children. Disabled people are lonely. And I have to believe one day we will be allowed the space to be the lover, the hero; to be flawed but not the stereotype of villainy. It needs saying again: to be part of what it is to be human – to be cute and sexy and messy as fuck!

To be in a position where I can tell our stories is a privilege I relish and a passion I will never lose. This is why I keep writing. I hope, dear reader, that you are glad.

Penny Pepper
March 2024

Editorial note: The first edition of this collection was written in the 1990s, and while it has been given an appropriate sensitivity read, I've changed these stories as little as possible to preserve their authenticity of the disabled narrative at the time.

Girls Wank Too

Tracey looked at her knickers, a pale pink colour with tiny blue teddy bears dancing on them. They were pulled down so that she could see the tufts of her tawny pubic hair. In her right hand, she held a long cotton bud, moistened with Vaseline. As she shot a fast glance at her very best friend Vanessa, she saw she was busy preparing the same. She smiled as a warm trembling sensation licked between her legs.

It had taken Tracey some time to settle in with the adults at Beechwood Rehabilitation and Physiotherapy Unit after a year in with the kids, and she could hardly believe what she was doing now.

There were lots of old ladies to get used to at one end. They smelt of pee and cigarettes, which was strange, as no one was allowed to smoke – only the staff, and they did it in a small special room. Fornication, she said, mostly at night when the girls lay stuffed in bed. The night carers wanted their bedtime to be even earlier of course, but Vanessa successfully led a posse to resist. One minute they were nagging that the girls must be grown up, that they couldn't be big babies – *then* they wanted them to go to bed at nine. It wasn't fair and showed how stupid they were.

Vanessa managed to get it extended to 9.30, and she was allowed up even later because she had homework to do, what with her exams coming up. And this was why she had the luxury of her own room at the end of the small corridor which linked the rectangular unit of eleven teenage girls with that of the unit for elderly women.

Everywhere was dirty white and peeling paint. It was one-third hospital, one-third care home, the final third a prison. The strict regime of physiotherapy to improve them – torture, the girls agreed – and rigorous schooling – very boring torture – made the days stretch thin and empty. Only in the early evening could the girls do their own thing, briefly.

Vanessa was a model of sophistication and adult knowledge – her clothes matched in colours that always looked great while Tracey never managed to get hers to stay still or adjust to her body how they should. Vanessa's breasts, too, belonged to the rest of her. Tracey wished hers would grow a bit and do the same.

It was her favourite thing to have Vanessa ask her to stay in her room, way past the 9.30 slap-down. They would gossip and giggle for hours until some grunt from the staff would barge in to shove Tracey off to bed. Some ragged care-nurse who moaned because Tracey needed help to get undressed. Weren't they working at a physio-rehab unit? Of disabled kids, lots like her in a wheelchair? What was Tracey doing – pretending? The staff get-out clause was always the independence thing, the drumming bang-bang insistence that you had to try hard to be normal. But instinct told most of the girls that the idea of normal imposed by the staff was a silly kind of normal, one they would never, ever reach.

Tracey sensed at this visit that Vanessa was in a different mood. She noticed how she looked especially grown-up and serious and was surprised when asked to help shove a small locker over in front of the door to the room, using the weight of their wheelchairs.

'Don't want those bastards interrupting,' Vanessa said, face firm. 'I want us to be left alone.'

At first Tracey assumed Vanessa might have some dope which they enjoyed previously cadged off one of the young porters. Tracey managed one gasp before giggling for hour, coughing so bad her throat was raw for days, then Sister Bracon made her take revolting pills afterwards.

'I'm being allowed home soon,' Vanessa announced, happy their barricade was secure.

Tracey gazed at the horrible blue colour of the walls and Nessa's *Hounds of Love* poster. These things happened. She wouldn't get soppy. The girls picked on her for that already. Even things on telly made her cry.

'You haven't said before. When did they tell you?'

'This afternoon. They're arranging things for me, at home. Then I can go. We'll write, won't we?'

'There's the new typewriter they let me use in the hobbies room. I heard they're getting a computer soon, too. Maybe you can phone sometimes?'

Vanessa turned her head, black hair settling on thin shoulders. 'Yeah, maybe, sometimes. You know my dad's a bit funny.'

Everyone's family was on the awkward side, there were always do's and don'ts and rules on who could be your friend. The girls didn't talk much about it, especially the problem families, which were best kept hidden in the safety of the shadows that fell over the Unit from the woods hugging around them.

'What have you shut us in here for tonight though?' Tracey laughed to change the subject. Vanessa was planning something.

The dark-haired girl giggled and looked away.

'It's a bit naughty. You must keep it a secret. The other girls are too silly to know. And it'd really show me up. I mean it.'

Tracey was startled. Vanessa wouldn't look at her.

'It's something you do, it feels really nice,' Vanessa continued, fidgeting by her bed.

'What? Come on,' Tracey said, moving her chair to be closer. 'Don't torment me.'

'Well first, I'm not a pervert or anything, you know that, don't you?'

'I know,' Tracey tutted. 'Just tell me.'

'What are your hands like at the moment? How far down can you reach? No, not quite all the way so we'll be clever.' Vanessa looked Tracey over with a calculating stare. 'Okay, try this first.'

She opened a drawer in her locker and pulled out a long cotton bud – really it was one of the things they used for throat swabs. All the girls sneaked them when they could, to do eye make-up.

Tracey frowned. 'Yeah?'

'You put it between your legs and rub. You know. Along your fanny.'

Tracey tittered and looked at her feet.

Vanessa stayed calm, and Tracey knew that Nessa was daring her to be stupid and start laughing.

'But what would you want to do that for?' Tracey whispered, keeping serious.

'Because it feels nice. More than nice. Amazing. I'll put a bit of Vaseline on it. That helps to move it about.'

'I can't do that now. It's embarrassing,' Tracey protested, pushing her wheelchair back. Yet despite her hot face and the tinge of shock, something, somewhere was intrigued. Tingles spread from her cheeks and she wanted to continue.

'I'm not going to stare at you doing it, silly. I know it seems a bit strange, but you will like it. Promise,' Vanessa's blue eyes shone. 'I'll give you the cotton bud and you can turn away. Use this blanket to cover yourself with if you want.'

'What if they catch us?' Tracey whispered again, as if They were listening right then to their dirty secret.

'They won't. They're not interested. Especially at night, you know that. Dr Boring is in the office and Nurse Fat Tits fancies him rotten. They'll be off into the smoking room if she has anything to do with it.'

Tracey detected layers to Vanessa's words but she held the long cotton bud, wondering. Outside it was a dark November night. There were lots of big trees pushing against the walls of the unit, fallen leaves everywhere. The trees made her feel safe and hidden as if they were on her side.

Vanessa put a cassette on, and the Jesus and Mary Chain's *Psychocandy* album began with a hiss from the small player. Tracey leant to one side, grabbed her handy helping stick and used it to try to edge down the corner of her knickers.

'Come on, aren't we soul sisters?' Vanessa was there, smiling again, helping as best she could with her own stiff fingers. They always joked that they were soul sisters who should have a blood-bonding ceremony. Hearing Vanessa say it again calmed Tracey's nerves.

After a bit of struggling between them, Tracey's knickers were pulled down enough to ease in the big cotton bud, oiled with helpful Vaseline.

'I won't look. Promise.' Vanessa tapped her arm and turned away. 'But I'll do it too so it's fair. Make sure it's right down, you know, right between your lips. Just ease it up and down, side to side.'

Tracey did as she was told and was shocked to feel tiny licks of sensation stir her private parts. She didn't think she had felt anything like it before, maybe a bit, sometimes in bed when she was tangled up with the covers high between her thighs and she had a feeling of wanting to push against them and not stop.

Yet this was different and she moved the cotton bud in a hard beat.

'Don't do it too quickly,' Vanessa spoke up from behind her. Tracey noticed her voice was different.

'It won't hurt me, will it, this rubbing?' Tracey exclaimed, but not stopping, no, she couldn't stop now.

'No. Don't let it make you sore. Put more Vaseline on.' Vanessa's words were short and rough as if speaking was hard. 'Slow the rubbing down if you can. It makes the feeling last longer before the end.'

'How will I know when the end is?' Tracey gasped as her uncooperative fingers clutched the thin stick, stroking it over and over her hungry awakened clitoris.

'Oh Tracey,' Vanessa was now hissing behind her. 'Oh, you… will… know. You will. Don't rush… but don't stop either.'

Tracey obeyed. There was a strong urge in her legs to push them apart. Her feet twitched with a peculiar cramp. As the wind outside stroked the bare branches against the big windows, she thought she was going to break apart. A delicious feeling rose and spread and shoved itself into her stomach and her chest. And now her tummy was tight, and yet deeper than her stomach, something else inside gripped. She stabbed the sticky slick cotton bud up and down hard, heat and pleasure consuming her body.

Tracey screeched as her first true orgasm hit. She cried again, a happy gasp, jabbing the bud, greedy to keep the sensation that smacked through her body.

'Shh-shhh,' Vanessa attempted to say but it came out in jolts. Then she was hissing again, 'Oh god, yes!'

Finally, she grunted, breathing heavily through her nose.

The bang on the door made them shriek. They scurried to cover themselves.

'What's the matter? Why won't this door open?' Nurse Fat Tits bellowed, pushing against the barricade.

'Sorry, Nurse Watling. Just dropped something,' Vanessa replied in a remarkably normal voice. 'We had to move the locker in front of the door to find it. No problems.'

There was a heavy pause as the handle was tried again.

'Hm. Okay. You get to bed now, Tracey. No arguments.'

'Yes, Nurse.' Tracey answered, trying not to giggle.

After hearing her thump away on her big flabby legs, they turned to face each other and laughed until they hurt.

'You know what we did, don't you?' Vanessa said when they were calmer. 'That's masturbation.'

'I thought only boys did that?' Tracey said, and pulled a disbelieving face.

'No, silly. Everyone can wank. There're lots of ways to make it even better. But you'll have to learn to be a bit quieter or they'll find out.'

'Is it like that when you do sex with a man?' Endless questions burst to be asked. 'Wanking is a sex thing, isn't it?'

'Yeah, what else did you think it was?' Vanessa laughed and lowered her voice. 'But all that stuff – with a bloke – is different too. They have to get their thing inside you, after all. I've been wondering about that. With our hips and all the rest, you think, no way. But there's more than one position. I've got a pen-pal who's done it and she can't move much at all. Her boyfriend lifts her legs up for her. She rests them on his body, and they do it that way.'

Tracey felt dizzy from information overload and stuttered for more. She tried to imagine sexual positions and pleasure and wanking all connected together but it was difficult. Especially as she hated most of the smelly, ratty boys she knew. Only a few of the Spanish porters made her wonder.

'I'm sick of being a virgin,' Vanessa confided, rolling her eyes. 'I'm going to think of how to do it as soon as I can.'

'Don't you want to fall in love first and do it with them?' Tracey tensed.

'Don't get all soppy on me. That's not real, Tracey. I mean, maybe I will fall in love when I do it, but I'm not marrying the first one. Definitely not.' She laughed.

Several minutes had passed since Fat Tits interrupted them. Tracey felt her cheeks burning and the sensation travelled down. She couldn't stop herself. 'Can't we wank again now?' she said, grinning.

*

Tracey really didn't intend to tell everyone, but Claire was a good friend too and knew lots of rude jokes. She claimed to know about wanking already but Tracey didn't believe her. After a while it seemed that several girls knew, and a weird kind of excitement co-existed with half-denial, as methods were found to share such a pleasure. A nasty moment occurred when the Unit's personal queen-bitch, Louise, challenged Vanessa. It was lunch and everyone was corralled to the long table, making it a time for maximum embarrassing exposure.

'You're a pervy lesbo, you are,' Louise sneered and the youngest girls trembled. 'We know what you get up to in that room.'

Louise flicked her beady stare to Tracey who swooned into the shame pit of her own stomach.

'You're just jealous you're so frigid,' Vanessa replied, looking Lou in the eye, 'and so ugly no one would want you anyway. Including me!'

No one expected Queen Bitch to burst into tears and to have to sit there because the staff said they were too busy to help her get up onto her crutches so she could escape.

Tracey noticed that Lou wasn't quite as cocky after that.

*

During the following weeks, Tracey had a small row with Vanessa for having spilled the beans, but they made up within a day, energised together by the secret that was now not so secret at all.

Vanessa instructed her in wanking variations. There were always obstacles to get around, like if your arms were short, or very weak and you couldn't reach or grip enough to keep hold of that thin cotton bud. Vanessa revealed she used a special spiral candle, with Vaseline. She said it felt fantastic to rub it slowly along your girl bits. And if it was a long candle, then you could reach easier.

There were upsets with some girls who were greedy for more and that made them silly, showing off on the unit, making jokes they thought were so adult. Tracey knew she was greedy, sneaking into the toilet maybe three times a day, soon with her own candle. Learning how to enjoy herself silently while keeping an ear very tensed for the slightest hint of a heavy staff footstep – no locks on the girl's loos, after all.

There were some difficult moments when Sian found out and wanted to do it. Tracey had let the secret slip to her too, but Sian's hands were very weak and couldn't grip. For a while they thought she wouldn't be able to, ever.

But when Vanessa heard, she shook her head, sighing. 'There is a way, we've got to work it out.' Neither Vanessa nor Tracey felt they could quite bring themselves to do it for her, it was such a secret, personal thing. Guiltily, they avoided Sian but she resolved the problem on her own by finding a friend, who she would not name, to wank her off. To everyone's surprise, it became obvious it was Louise, but no one said anything, it didn't feel right, when so many of the Unit were enjoying themselves.

Poor Claire, who was a bit dotty, lost the plot, sitting in her wheelchair, shoving pens in her pants, not able to fish them out. Vanessa told Tracey she had seen her go redder than you could imagine when one of the religious carers watched them drop from her undies as she helped to undress her. The girls teased all the time, don't borrow a pen off Claire, it'll smell fishy.

*

Time moved on a roundabout of gossipy whispers that most of the girls on the Unit were masturbating, and too soon it came to the night before Vanessa was going home. Tracey moped in Nessa's room, noting that all the posters were down. Even her envied spread of make-up was packed. Tracey felt the trees were too quiet, not tapping on the windows. Her eyes burned but she would not, no, would *not* cry.

'I've got a present for you,' Vanessa grinned and handed her a plastic bag.

Inside was a box. It contained a long creamy plastic implement that had ridges at one end, tapering to a point. Tracey examined it eagerly but her face showed her confusion.

'It's a vibrator,' Vanessa explained quickly. 'My friend sent it to me through the post, the one I told you about who's had sex. This makes wanking easier, although it's a bit noisy. You should mention it to

Claire one day, if you can. It would help her out too. Someone could just put it there for her.'

'Have you tried one yet?' Tracey rolled it over in her hands.

'Naturally, but it buzzes. I've done it in bed in this room with lots of blankets on me in case they hear. Really good it was. I can't explain how it feels. Intense.'

Tracey felt the little stir between her legs that was so familiar. She wondered when she could try the vibrator.

'My friend calls hers the Milky Bar Kid,' Vanessa said, but fell silent.

They both knew that now they faced only the exchange of slow letters and rare phone calls, not much to look forward to.

Later, Vanessa found a boyfriend and she told Tracey about doing It for real and how, after a bash or two, it felt fantastic. But it took a long time to adjust to Nessa not being on the Unit and Tracey could do nothing much more than stare at the shedding leaves and listen to the gathering winds of winter.

The Milky Bar Kid stayed silent in her handbag.

*

A day came when there was a huge incident. Claire was caught wanking in the toilet with Louise's candle. Tracey hoped they were remembering to wash it, and thought it was quite funny because the staff were so embarrassed, even more than the girls. They were all sent to bed even earlier, and Sister Monster McMurray stood in the middle of the Unit, huffing and red as she stared furiously at the floor.

'This depraved activity must stop. It is not nice for girls. We don't know who started it and it no longer matters. You girls are merely storing up trouble for yourselves when you are older. You cannot expect to have… desires… in view of your limitations. And I have to be cruel to be kind and say that men… being as they are, will not find you attractive. Do not torment yourselves by awakening these instincts. We hope this is the end of the matter.'

Some of the girls tittered. Tracey boiled with rage. McMurray Mint wasn't even married, she was shrivelled and old, a spinster.

Tracey didn't believe any of their crap, she refused it. It was more stupid rubbish from them. She found consolation quickly. Although it was chilly, in her coat and with the shielding blanket, she wheeled in her own methodical manner and pace to the edge of the wood, enjoying the smell of the leaves.

With the Milky Bar Kid nestled in secret – if difficult – preparation between her eager labia, she felt for the switch and closed her eyes.

Postcards For Jean

A small blue budgerigar made keen *ch-ch* noises and moved from one leg to the other in its large clean cage. Voices from the street in front of Jean's room came laughing inside. She froze, looking for the source. Two people hung by the gate and onto each other, and even the voile could not stop her from recognising one of them.

'Fiona's home.' Jean looked at the budgie but felt drawn back to the gate. 'Let's see how long it takes her to get through the door today, naughty young thing.'

As a breeze tugged the lilac voile slouching in the window, Jean turned her wheelchair and moved away from the high table where neat piles of postcards lay in assorted stacks.

'Getting a bit nippy, Roger. Must that window shut.'

The voile continued to billow. She hated net curtains but Imogen said she had to have privacy, you could gawp right into her room otherwise. Jean couldn't remember when the thing went up and she still missed seeing into the street without its dulling interference. But Imogen was in charge and that was the end of the matter.

A fresh blast came through the small window and threatened the heaps of postcards as the voile reared high. Jean gathered them, muttering under her breath.

'Hi, Auntie Jean. Is mum in?' Fiona tapped on the window as she spoke.

Jean swung her power wheelchair to see Fiona, dark hair in long bunches, broad pretty face pressed close to the glass. A blue stud in her lower lip flashed as she grinned.

'Yes, I think so,' Jean replied brightly then added, 'Come and see me later, can you? Please?'

Jean realised the young woman was gone before her sentence had ended.

She cursed the voile and tried again to put the postcards into some kind of order.

Over many years the family sent them to her, at first from Britain. Torquay, Great Yarmouth, Minehead, Hastings. There would be a startled black cat in the centre of country cottages, beaches with stick-like bathers bearing up on unforgiving pebbles. Slowly the cards became exotic. Spain and the Canaries first, then France and Portugal. The latest batch included America and Thailand. Fiona declared she wanted to live in Thailand.

The problem was how to store them. Jean owned a proper postcard album, a very nice one from Len last Christmas. For such a quiet man he always made a big effort with his presents. Jean wondered if it was some kind of wordless rebellion against being married to Imogen.

But should she store them chronologically? Or by region? She shuffled them around, hoping for inspiration. A card poked out its presence, being larger than the rest. Jean stared at it and laughed.

'Roger, can you believe it? One of those silly proposals Nigel had a phase of sending me.'

She knew Nigel from the art class and it felt like they had been going forever. The card was a reproduction of Monet's 'Water Lilies,' and Nigel had printed his message in capitals, a result of the constant teasing she did about his scrawled handwriting.

JEANIE, JEANIE, LAUGHING JEANIE. MARRY ME NOW AND SAVE ME FROM DREARY MISERY.

'Daft he is.' She gazed at it for several silent minutes then quickly pulled another pile closer to sift through. Soon she found another one of Nigel's, this time Van Gogh's 'Sunflowers'.

JEANIE I MEAN IT. SO DON'T BE A MEANIE, JEANIE. MARRY ME AND BE MINE-Y.

Putting them together, she wondered how many he had sent over the years. When had he stopped? She didn't want to marry him. After all, she didn't love him. That was preposterous, two ageing cripples fooling themselves. The whole idea of marriage, of its intimacies and duties was surely revolting, or at least completely ridiculous.

She picked up Nigel's cards. They really did deserve a special place all on their own.

The door to her room burst open and Fiona flew in.

Jean jumped and thought, I wish she would knock, Imogen should tell her – but she smiled and welcomed the kiss planted warmly on her head.

'These postcards, Auntie Jean. They're fantastic. Some are real museum pieces, aren't they?' She picked up one of Margate, families frozen in loud sixties fashions.

'Seeing as I'm such an antique, I suppose?' Jean said, relieved Fiona hadn't seen the ones from Nigel.

'No, I didn't mean it like that, really. You're not as old as mother dearest, after all.'

'Was she in?'

'Nope. Gran is though and off with the fairies as usual.'

There was a pause. Jean stared at a postcard from New Zealand. She wanted to ask Fiona who it was that had come to the gate with her, who she kissed and wound her young eager body around. A fact not dimmed by the waving voile.

'Auntie, can you lend me a fiver?' Fiona looked down at her pale blue nail varnish, frowning when she saw a chip. 'I had a last minute rush at work. Forgot to go to the cash point.'

'You are naughty,' Jean answered but began to move towards the purse on the table. Fiona owed her £15 already this month. 'What's it for this time?'

'I've got to dash out again soon, have a date. Thought I'd get myself some fish and chips to keep me going. If you give me a tenner, I could run back with some for you, if you like.'

Jean declined the offer and knew Fiona expected her to decline.

As Jean opened her purse, concentrating to steady the tremors in her fingers, Fiona jumped up from her bed, bright face smiling, hair bunches swaying. With a fast light hand, she took the note and kissed Jean again.

'I love you Auntie Jean. You're fabulous.'

It was only after Fiona had flown that Jean remembered the draught from the open window.

Later she would overhear the guileless chatter on the stairway in the hall, as Fiona showed off new earrings to her mother. Bought that afternoon, before the shops shut. With her last fiver.

Jean cooed at Roger, hating the tears that threatened to splash onto the sea in a harbour scene at Tenby.

*

The next day Jean started the routine off with an old movie on a Sky channel before attempting a new method of storing the postcards. Just after one, Imogen brought down a sandwich lunch from upstairs.

'Everything all right? Do you need the toilet? What time do you want dinner brought down? We're off out around 6.30-ish, something on at Len's work. So it'll be salad only, I'm afraid. Or you could eat something hot later?' The woman was tall with a large, thick middle and her words stuttered out in one long string.

'Immsie, let me speak then,' Jean said, voice shrill. 'Can you shut that window, please? It's been bothering me all night.'

'I don't know why you had it open in the first place. I knew it would be too cold, I told you.' Imogen moved to it immediately. 'And Jean. Please don't call me Immsie. I've let it drop for a while, I know it's a small thing but please try to remember. I'm Imogen.'

'I'm not arguing about it, I forget,' Jean said and watched her sister move around the room, straightening the bed, tugging the hateful voile, peering at Roger and looming over her postcards.

'Leave them.' She ordered, throat tightening.

'Silly things.' The older woman twisted sour lips. 'Why on earth you keep messing around with them, I don't know.' Her hands hovered dangerously closer to them. 'Look at that! Benidorm, can you believe it? It was such a shabby place.'

'Least you went,' Jean said quietly, regretting it at once.

Imogen swung round, frowning heavy eyebrows into a challenge.

'No. Sorry. We are not starting on that one again. Really, Jean. I know things get to you, stuck in this room with only a silly bloody bird for company, but what do you expect me to say? We do our best. We got Sky TV put in down here didn't we?'

Jean stared at the TV gently burbling adverts in the background, her jaw locking.

'No I don't need the toilet and I'll have salad at six. Thank you very, very much.' Jean didn't look up.

Imogen shrugged, shook her head and slammed the door as she left. The noise startled the budgerigar into a twittering alarm.

'Shh, Roger, it's only Imogen showing off,' Jean moved her chair over to the cage that took up one corner of the table, positioned so she could slide a comforting finger between the bars.

When he fell back to his normal soft clucking, she returned to the postcards and resisted an urge to throw them on the floor.

'Maybe they are silly,' she whispered. 'They didn't really mean anything when they sent them, either.'

The TV lured her away from sudden decisions and they stayed in forlorn, neglected heaps, the startled black cat from Swanage no threat to Roger.

*

At six Danny brought down the salad dinner and she let him watch cartoons so he would stay, vaguely chatting, and then be there to help her clean out Roger's cage when she had eaten.

She knew he saw this as a serious honour, biting his lip to steady his big, eight-year-old hands.

'Why don't you get Roger someone to play with Auntie?'

'They might not get on. He's quite old now too. He probably wouldn't like it.'

'What about a girlfriend though? They could lay eggs and stuff. That'd be cool.'

Jean laughed. 'Roger's definitely too old for making eggs with a girlfriend.'

Danny was silent for a few moments, carefully sweeping out the contents from the floor of the cage. 'Girls have eggs, don't they? I mean, you know. Ladies. Even Fiona. Do you have them too, Auntie?'

Roger perched on the arm of Jean's wheelchair. He made little clicking noises when she stroked his head and she loved the times he was free from his confinement, when she could touch him.

'I suppose I must have eggs somewhere,' she said cautiously. She knew Imogen would have told them all the facts of life when they were nippers. Not what she would have done, of course. But they weren't her children, and she had been slapped in the face with that reminder many times.

A pleased smile stretched across Danny's face as he held the door of Roger's cage open so Jean could ease the bird back in.

'That's it, safe and sound,' she coaxed, chilled with guilt as he fluttered behind bars again.

Roger seemed less perturbed than she was. He ruffled his wings, immediately pecking at the fresh seed in his tray.

'Fiona's got a new boyfriend,' Danny announced. 'Mum said this one's serious. There will be news, Mummy said.'

'News?' Jean queried. Cool air breathed around her neck but the voile was still and sulky against the glass. 'What news?'

'Mum told Dad he's not our type. What's that mean, Auntie?'

Danny's brown eyes widened as he waited for her answer.

Jean looked away and focused on the disorganised postcards on the table.

'I'm not sure, Danny. I'm afraid Aunties don't always know everything, even Auntie Jean. You'll have to ask Mummy.'

'Yeah, s'pose,' he began slowly. 'But she might tell me I was being nosey.' He leant to one side and began to scuff the carpet with his trainer.

'Maybe we are being nosey, a bit. You go back upstairs now. I'm sure Fiona will tell us more when she's ready.'

She could see Danny was bored already with talking about Fiona. He grabbed the dinner tray and bounded to the door with a cheerful goodbye. Jean listened as he banged up the stairs that connected her small bed-sit to her sister's flat above.

A green Thai Buddha stared up at her from a crumpled postcard as she moved back to the table.

'What's my Fiona been up to now?' she sighed, casting a glance at Roger out of habit, aware that only sad old women talked to themselves. 'It is about time she settled down.'

*

It took three weeks before Jean managed to organise even half of the postcard collection, boredom creeping over her as the winter nights closed in. The messages written were whining repetitions: *weather too hot, weather too cold. Beach is rather dirty. Food terrible.*

It appeared the family had spent endless trips complaining. From Skegness to San Francisco, there would be a card with a grumble.

'I think I'd like Spain,' she lifted her head to look out of the window but the stern cold of a November morning kept the light bleak. All she could see was the faint outline of the gate muted by the lilac against the glass.

There had been one holiday with Imogen and the family. The weather had been predictably poor and they had underestimated how much room would be needed in the car, for her wheelchair in the boot, and her unbending legs in the rear seat. Her mother, mentally sharp in those days, had insisted Imogen, Len and Baby Fiona use the bus.

Jean shuddered as she remembered Bognor and the lift at the drab hotel which always shut on her ankles, the bathroom too small for her wheelchair, and her mother somehow conjuring up an ancient, stained commode which she delayed using to the point of extreme pain. People staring everywhere. She was an alien pushed into an alien world with children pointing and old people shrieking, 'What's wrong with her face?', 'Why can't she walk?' as they went by, craning their heads back to gawp.

Imogen made a scene about everything and Jean told her she hated being on holiday with them anyway, she was not a child and did not like being pushed around like one. Imogen screamed that she was an ungrateful cow.

Jean never went again and no one asked her. Her mother – then Imogen – arranged extra home-care when they were away and most of the time Jean grew to enjoy the solitude.

'I must have got some blank postcards of Bognor,' she mused and wondered where they could be.

Roger chirped, unashamed of any conversation he had with himself.

Jean checked the time. The young evening home-carer, Michelle, was due any minute, with her rough hands and bulldozing efficiency. Jean would be pushed through the care conveyor belt. Stripped, scrubbed, toileted and watered by nine, able to read for maybe an hour before she became too tired to hold the book.

At the moment she was reading David Attenborough's 'Life on Earth,' a large hardback which darling Fiona had picked up for her in a charity shop.

Its weight overcame her at after eleven, and she let it slip to the side on the bed, clicking off the lamp on the flex switch to fall asleep quickly.

She awoke in the dark in some confusion and heard a low and regular moaning, interjected with whispers and soft laughter. Her senses flooded awake to strain sense from these sounds, which seemed inexplicably nearby.

The soft female voice was familiar but she could not place it. There seemed to be a certain rhythm to it and when she heard a man's voice speak over the pattern of moaning, a terrible realisation struck. The moaning, sexual moaning, became more intense, interrupted with insistent hushing and a hissed, *Quiet, Fiona darling.*

The man groaned too and a faint creak of bed springs began to beat time.

With cheeks burning in the darkness, Jean tried to bury her head further under the duvet. Should she call out? Why wouldn't Roger wake up and make a noise?

Fiona's pleasure continued to delve beneath the virginal bastion of Jean's duvet. She screwed her eyes up and began to whimper. When would they stop, bloody rutting animals?

Imogen insisted *she* must keep the spare room downstairs for guests – Jean was scarcely allowed to peer into it. Now it was being used by Imogen's daughter, in secret no doubt, with some bloody man, Jean chafed, as tears stung her eyes.

The moaning carried on, slowing down, changing pace. Jean could hear the man whispering again, then the bed would start to squeak with a quickening tempo. She found herself helplessly drawn to listen, to wonder what he was doing, this mysterious male, grunting so much pleasure from Fiona.

Their intimate sounds captured her whole attention as the bed made its tell-tale echo and revealed the pace of movement. Hot and confused, Jean's mind meandered to wonder what position they were in. She'd seen sex on TV on late night movies. It was always so athletic, the women straddling the men, or the men lying on top of the women and there was a lot of moving about. She found herself imagining Fiona pressed onto the bed, her beau grinding down. Fiona's dark brown hair flying like ravens across the white snow of the pillow, her dancing eyes half closed, smooth young lips parted to utter the distinctive sounds, as he, anonymous, pushed himself into her.

The creak of the bed quickened and the blood in Jean's cheeks stirred. Her hands shook under the bedclothes. She stopped thinking and only listened, tongue dry from her open mouth. The man's grunts became harder as the tempo increased, Fiona's gasps weaving an accompaniment.

Jean began to tremble and the clenching in her chest was unbearable. The man gave a strange, guttural cry, the bed squeaking in a mad stutter and suddenly there was silence.

*

Morning strained through the darkness with a weak pale sun. Jean went through the usual routine with her favourite morning home-carer, Dora, who assisted to bathe and dress her. Dora was a big square woman with small, gentle hands, and a rich Jamaican accent despite living in London for over 30 years.

Jean's words mumbled from unwilling lips as she tried to find a way to tell Dora about the previous night. Dora would joke about that sort of thing but Jean feared her own attempts would erupt in a torrent of disgust. Even though she did not know if it was disgust she felt.

'You not well today?' Dora paused while combing Jean's hair. 'You more quiet than usual. An' you going to your classes?'

Jean nodded and sighed. She had half-forgotten it was Wednesday, the day when the Community Bus would arrive around ten to take her to the Disability Activities Centre, where she did art. A day out. A change of walls. A different smell.

'Dora, do you miss your husband?' The sentence came struggling out and her face flushed hot.

Dora laughed and waved her hands. 'That a strange question all of a sudden. I miss him more sometimes than other times. I miss him in me arms, keeping me warm, he were a big strong man before the cancer got him.'

Jean looked at the window and saw faint figures walking past. The voile looked like an overdone wash that she had been taught at art classes.

'Do you let your Ian, you know, do things with girls, in your house?' she whispered, shivering with embarrassment.

'Another strange question, Jean. I don't let him do what he wants with his girlfriends when I'm in the house. But when I not there, I know he get up to things. He a big boy now. We all do that when we young.'

Jean looked at herself in the mirror on the small dressing table. Dora had made her brown greying hair look tidy. What should she make of the reflection, gawping at her with timid eyes and thin tight lips, the way her face was? So different to everyone else.

'Now I go and get your breakfast from your sister,' Dora said, and went upstairs. Jean took the chance to go along the hall to peer into the guest room. The door was open yet the bed was pristine.

*

Nigel was at the centre before her, as usual, his speed a result of having his own car with a wheelchair lift. Every week there would be a joke about whisking her away in his carriage. The last marriage proposal had been so long ago, she wondered now if she had imagined it, but today she ached to have him say it again.

They sat at tables, some at easels with paints besides them. Jean saw how grey his hair was and it made her smile.

'Christmas soon Jeanie,' he said, gliding his chair to face her. 'What are you doing this year? Don't tell me, you start on that luxury world cruise on 20th December, don't you?'

'I'll start with New York, meander around New England then back to my sumptuous cabin for the next leg. To sunny parts,' she laughed.

'I'd take you to New York, Jeanie.' Nigel looked at her intently. 'You think I'm joking, but I'm not. It's possible, Jeanie. There's companies that do that sort of thing for disabled people. A few of the chaps here have done it.'

'Nigel, don't be silly,' she sighed, inundated with visions of stained commodes and steely jawed *elevators* snapping at her ankles. 'I know you want to cheer me up all the time, but I don't need it, really.'

'I've never forgotten what you've told me, that dreadful sister you've got. Taking your car – no, it is your car Jeanie, your mobility benefit bought the damn thing. And when did they last take you anywhere in it?'

She held her paintbrush in mid-air. 'I never really ask to go anywhere, do I?'

'Not surprisingly. It could all be different if you wanted it.'

'Nigel, please. I'm too old.' She dabbed the paintbrush on the page and spread a watery line of red across the empty white.

When it was lunch break, she yearned to tell Nigel about the night before but the thought of any discussion with him mentioning sex scared her nervous words away.

'Jeanie, you aren't your normal self.' He nudged her drink towards her. 'You are totally preoccupied and I want to know with what.'

'Things at home. You're right, I should change, do my own thing more. But I'm past all the effort. I want a nice easy life.'

'I don't believe you. We've come here for… what? Over ten years? I started at this class a little while before you did. When I first saw you, I knew you were different. You had a bit of spark.'

'You're impossible,' she smiled, picking up her drink. 'And misguided.'

*

Once the Community Bus dropped her off, she drove her chair through the shared front door to find Danny, looking red-eyed and forlorn, hanging onto the handle to her room.

'Auntie, auntie,' he wailed. 'Don't go in yet. Don't look. Roger's gone to heaven.'

'What?' She pushed forward, ramming the door open. Inside her room, Imogen stared down at the table. Roger was a pile of motionless feathers.

Jean's chest constricted, face fixed in stone.

'You killed him.'

Imogen stepped back, white and startled.

'Jean, no, don't be silly. Danny found him, didn't you?' The boy nodded, snivelling.

She charged her chair forwards.

'Jean, I know you loved this little budgie,' Imogen said. 'We'll get you a new one. He can be another Roger.'

'Don't patronise me. Leave me alone. Get out.'

Imogen left, biting her mouth together, waving her hands uselessly. Danny ran out too, shocked out of crying by Jean's raised voice.

Alone, she scooped up the bird and cupped it to her body. His feathers were soft and she realised she had never been able to touch him this much before. His eyes were shut, his head limp.

She wept intermittently, tears dribbling onto her clothes and his feathers. There was a gentle knock and Fiona came in.

She rushed to Jean's side and stroked her hair, which made Jean cry more.

'It's all right Auntie, please don't. Please. You'll make me cry too.'

'I know you all think I'm pathetic and stupid. It's a bird, a silly little bird,' Jean trembled and attempted to find a tissue from her sleeve.

Fiona found a box and pulled a few out for her.

'I don't think that, I don't. Mum doesn't understand, she's not an animal person. Me and Danny do. Oh, he's so upset. He really is. He doesn't really understand about things dying yet.'

'Yes, of course, Danny loved Roger too.' Jean rubbed her eyes, still clutching the bird.

'Why don't you let Mum bring you down some soup? She's worried about you.'

'It's not about Roger,' Jean began, her voice almost under control. 'There's something else.'

'You heard us, didn't you?' Fiona stood up. Her voice was small, trying to hide in the corner. 'I am *so* embarrassed. And really sorry. It was selfish. Look, I'm blushing.'

With dark hair flying she turned back to kneel by Jean's chair. 'The thing is Auntie, and you're the first to know. We're getting married.'

Jean stopped crying. 'Married? When? To him?' She threw her gaze to the spare room.

'Yes, to him, David. I love him so much. I never thought I'd go for marriage, but now he's asked, it's the only thing I want to do.'

'Yes, you must, then,' Jean whispered and tried to smile as she imagined the house empty of Fiona.

'I haven't told anyone else yet, you're honoured.' She moved to kiss Jean's head. 'Auntie, what do you want to happen to Roger? We have to do something, don't we.'

'Please don't let Imogen put him in the dustbin,' she pleaded. 'He was merely a budgerigar, I know, but he kept me company. I won't treat him like rubbish.'

'Me and Danny will bury him in the garden, that'll help Danny too.' Fiona leant forward and held her long fingers open for the dead bird. 'Maybe Dad can sort out a ramp over those steps, then you can be there too.'

Reluctantly, Jean let him go into her strong young hands. She stroked his head a few times, unable to speak. Fiona lifted him up and held the tiny animal against her chest.

'I'll come back soon, I promise. And maybe I'll bring David to meet you.'

Jean nodded and tried to stop the tears. Fiona lowered her gaze to the table, the postcards laying like forgotten children waiting for homes.

'Oh Auntie! What a lovely proposal!' Fiona said, waving a card. 'Why didn't you say yes? I met Nigel once, I think, when you had the open day at the centre. He was a real gentleman.'

Jean didn't answer as Fiona shut the door quietly.

Jean realised she had no excuse to speak aloud. But she did anyway, to the ghost of Roger. 'Why didn't I say yes? Why?'

*

By eleven the next morning, Dora removed Roger's cage. There could be no new Roger.

In the post, a card came from Nigel: *You were quite miserable yesterday, and wouldn't tell me why. But I've lapsed in my commitment. Jeanie, marry me and that Christmas in New York will happen.*

She felt dulled by wondering – as always – what he saw in her, what it was that she could not see.

Finding a pen and paper, she started to write a letter. Somehow she had to explain things, even if Nigel would think her stupid and childish.

She began by explaining her soppy decision to call the budgie Roger. Andrew Rogers had been their art tutor some years ago. Jean quickly decided to fall in love with him. Youngsters would call it a crush. Daft, unrequited love. But it had been a good feeling, the rush at seeing him every week, pouring over his eyes, his firm, swift legs and dark good looks. Could Nigel compete with him; with her daydreams?

Jean looked down at the rapid scrawl and with her hands setting off into sudden shakes, she screwed it up the best she could.

'Fiona's right. Why shouldn't I? Really, Roger, why not?'

Nigel always put his phone number at the top of his cards. Jean turned her chair to the side of the table where the phone was positioned for ease of reach. As she lifted the handset to dial, her breath quickened.

Behind the still lilac voile she saw Fiona and David move to the gate, holding hands.

Fooling for Charlie

The sun was bright, the rain had stopped and it was looking like it might be spring. Richard wanted to be out in it, to be clean and fresh like the shining London streets.

He felt twitchy with quality skunk hollering in his inside pocket. A little recreational puff was one thing, but this was in the cause of unrequited love. At least, he would call it that for now and gloss over the lecherous instincts he had towards darling Charlie, today looking ripe and gift-wrapped in tight denim.

His fingers kept probing the pocket hot with drugs. He pondered how funny it was to end up scoring the shit from his cleaner, such a pale, timid little thing from Albania. Charlie would love it and he would regale her with the story at the first opportunity.

He waited at the bar while the women stayed at the table. They were in a cramped little drinking hole to the north of King's Cross. Richard could hear Charlie and Mel laughing about the décor, the purple walls and clashing maroon swashes at the windows. Oh God, it was so tacky, they agreed, Charlie's voice the loudest, her head bobbing as she spoke, a colourful bird flouncing her plumage. And the punters? Trendy scum, wouldn't piss on a crip unless you paid them.

Trying to appear resigned, Richard turned his wheelchair to a different position and tapped the bar, but again, the barman failed to register his presence. It was something to note, to file, to remember – along with all the other times he had felt invisible. Anger could come later, maybe, if he felt like doing something about it. But today was really a day for being with Charlie; for absorbing Charlie. As he waited, a blast of new sunshine came cheekily through the entrance to the bar and Richard wished he could snatch its courage, to do something straightforward. Like simply asking Charlie out.

A pretty barmaid peered over the ridiculously high counter. She smiled, nervous, brightly made-up eyes not holding his.

'Three pints of Blackthorn, please,' he grinned too much, wanting to say something witty and perfect to put her at ease. Yet there were only so many reassuring clichés to draw on, after all, when ordering your booze.

'You getting those drinks, Rich, honey?' Charlie called over in clear, mellow tones. Richard detected the charming tinge of an accent that wasn't London – there was an inflection of Up North, perhaps. The bad-mannered bang of bland jazz jumped from the speakers. Richard nodded, an absent-minded gesture to the barmaid and Charlie – loath to throw in his voice to compete with the noise so far from their table, where five of them sat. Jeff, lean and disgustingly cool in a low-backed sporty wheelchair, angled one side of Charlie. Mel – Charlie's best mate – big and brown-haired in a high-tech tank of a power chair sat on the other side. Tim, the skinny joker of their gathering, was there too, with guide dog Hobby, napping by his feet.

Charlie smiled as Richard returned, her slow wide half-grin a Mona-Lisa gone sassy. Every time it disturbed him. Mel was already lolling forward, gesturing away three empty pint glasses with rolling eyes.

'She's off. She'll hit the table soon.' Charlie was droll, but Richard sensed her concern.

'Oh well,' he started feebly, 'you enjoy it though, don't you, Mel?'

'Not half as much as a line or two.' She swayed and strands of brown hair fell into her plump face. 'Better than official, um, medication.'

He began to tap his fingers, pretending to be casual – when really Mel pissed him off with that shit. Once they had all been to some party, and there she was, a bag of the damn stuff perky as a Pekinese on her lap.

'I won't use a rolled fiver, of course. Impossible without fiddling from a PA, and you never know whose snot might be on it,' Mel cackled, then slurped at the new glass of cider the surly barmaid brought over.

Jeff was sitting at the end corner of the chunky, wooden table – not friendly to wheelchair-users. It had long planks near floor level that connected at each leg. Richard wondered why Jeff always sat there, his foot-plates chipping off bits of wood as he attempted to get closer. But then, he was near enough to Charlie to meditate on a pair of breasts that – whatever niceties you used – were impossible not to notice.

Jeff was slim and athletic, a true crip sports jock type, Richard mused, not able to throw off agitation which jumped about in his head like the mediocre jazz. Jeff had the set of attributes Richard supposed would appeal: a guy who knew what clothes suited him, who was always relaxed with women, cracking jokes and leering in a way they never seemed to notice. Richard allowed seedy envy to swill with the cider in his guts, with side glances to his beloved Charlie.

Tim's dog caused the regular diversion and Richard admitted to further envy as the barmaid crouched down to pet it, cooing platitudes about 'blind dogs' and bravery (dog and Tim he supposed), but took a crumb of comfort while relishing in some neutral corner of himself, the fine curve of a female buttock unusually close to his view.

Two personal assistants belonging to their group lurked nearby, some reading, others clutching drinks. When a greasy middle-aged barman sidled up, Richard saw the warning signs flicker in glances between Mel and Charlie. The group made little signals to each other and everyone stopped speaking.

'You ladies very good, caring for these poor people. So beautiful, too.' The barman began, in stilted English, hovering near to Charlie's PA, Yvonne. 'I like to treat you to drink. Your work difficult, eh, being a carer?'

Yvonne shifted back from him, looking at Charlie for help. 'I'm not exactly a carer, really. That woman there is my boss.'

'No, they aren't carers, they're PAs and they probably get paid more than you do,' Charlie said, clearly, without a trace of anger, adding quietly. 'You see some of us actually find one fucking mother enough, and we don't go out of our way to hire more.'

The barman looked at them sulkily. 'What harm is there in them having a little drink? You should appreciate these lovely girls more.'

'Look, we don't want a drink. Thank you. We are working and very happy, okay? Please leave us alone.' Mel's worker, Lyn, spoke up.

'Fine, fine. I'm trying to be friendly, that's all.' He stood there for a second, flummoxed, scratching his ear, walking off swearing under his breath.

They all hunched down into stifled laughter. 'Oh fuck, why do we always get them?' Charlie hissed.

Richard gazed out of the tall French windows, which opened onto a balcony above the grubby Regent's Canal below. Plump London ducks idled on the lazy flow, squabbling intermittently. The occasional colourful long boat drifted by on a smug peacefulness, soft with laughter and secrets as perfect beautiful people tinkled glasses and preened in the indiscriminate sun. Richard puffed his cheeks up and dismissed them, as he blew out the bored air from his lungs. The trilling jazz stopped molesting the speakers and the group immediately filled the silence with easier conversation.

'I'm bloody bored shitless,' Mel slurred between mouthfuls as one of the PAs assisted with a constant stream of soggy chips into her mouth. 'That doughnut manager is getting on my tits. He doesn't like us *cripples* in his trendy bar and I don't like him, his crap food or his slimy barmen either. I think he needs a fucking social worker, an assessment to sort *his* attitude problems out.'

Everyone cackled.

'Why don't we go somewhere else?' Charlie suggested and looked at Richard.

Tim could use the tube and a handful of buses were accessible. But only for one wheelchair-user at a time, so there would be no mass exodus that way. Richard felt relieved he had his own transport.

'I'll come with you, if that's okay?' Charlie kept her gaze on him, voice low and focused. 'Your WAV's got room for two wheelchairs, hasn't it?'

This was unexpected. He knew she wanted her goodies of course, weighty and eager in his pocket, but the sun now roared in his head to think he was getting Charlie in his car.

'Yeah, fine. Let me finish my sad, single pint. And we've got to decide where we're off to.' He spoke quickly, hands gripping his glass too hard. 'We could do something, together I mean. Regent's Park might be good. The sun's out now. It'd be really laid back after this place.'

She gazed into him with her big brown eyes. Time froze as he felt his yearnings being assessed and considered. He looked away into the dregs of his drink.

'Oh Richard, that'd be cool,' she sighed at last.

He twisted and flushed. Spring was pert and wagging its tail inside him.

Charlotte, he wanted her on his lap, those breasts around his face–

'Deserting us together, are we?' Mel's voice staggered on a wavery alcoholic haze. 'That'll get the gossip going.'

'Oh fuck, who cares about gossip?' Charlie's eyes swung back, shining with disapproval.

'Okay, keep the toupee on.' Mel pulled a comical face. 'Seeing as us oppressed crips can't be choosy about transportation, I'm off to a bar around the corner which has access and booze. I'll go on wheel and foot, as it were.'

Jeff moved away from his prime breast-watching position and winked at Richard. 'Lucky bunny today, aren't we?'

Richard reared on hind legs, claws sharp. Jeff was a mate but he wouldn't gloat over this sudden gift of time with Charlie. Not yet.

'Don't know what you mean, exactly.' He hoped his voice was as insubstantial as the light breeze.

'Rich, this endless lusting for the delicious Charlie is not good for a man. Go for it, my son. You two should get it on, at the earliest.'

Richard skipped cautious eyes to Charlie who was organising assistance from Yvonne. An urge overwhelmed him to fall into a crude ramble with Jeff, to let go of the tiring calculations of effort to simply be talking to Charlie. He wanted to say to Jeff, yep it's true, I want Charlie, fucking hell, I want her. A one-off fuck doesn't come into it... but it would be a start.

He found his mouth wouldn't co-operate and his tongue rolled up into silence. There was something more. Charlie was not a cheap fairground prize you took home to enjoy one night and discard on the next. Maybe he didn't know what he wanted, exactly, apart from the obvious. Maybe the knowing would come after the obvious – if he ever got to that.

'No comment, then?' Jeff caught his eye once more and grinned. 'Well, she does have great tits, eh? Whatever else you might be thinking, I know you're thinking that.'

Richard put his hands on the wheels of his chair and began to move away. He shrugged a frosty farewell to Jeff and moved towards Charlie who was ready to leave.

Richard eased into the perfect environment of his car like a fish diving into the water. The Mercedes Vito was a prize won through a hard slog in his boring job for the bank where he worked as senior admin officer, in charge of IT. As they went through the business of waiting for the wheelchair lift to come out – to get inside and be clamped into place – he was pleased to remember that Charlie had a dodgy PC that he could promise to look at. As soon as possible.

'I hope it stays sunny,' she said, now beside him. 'I need to get away from those bar staff arseholes back there. And the racket. The park should be peaceful.'

'At least we can leave the Vito for three hours.' He hoped he didn't sound too breathless and idiotic but he wanted to talk to her, to keep the path ahead empty of obstruction.

'Do you have to get home by any particular time?' Charlie's voice played into the breeze.

'Not really.' Richard shook his head, guiding the Vito into a line of thick traffic. He answered carefully. 'I can leave the rest of the day open-ended.' He thought of home, a one-bedroomed council flat that was almost entirely pale beige.

He cringed always to think of the pale beige, but decorating was something he had never organised. Charlie's flat was modern with chic Ikea rugs, lots of blue and chrome, always minimalist flowers in a vase.

'No rush then,' Charlie grinned.

Richard pushed the car on as quickly as was safe. He told himself to ease down.

Charlie was never difficult company, she was a *mate*, whatever else, and the park with its flat accessible pathways and entertaining squirrels would be a perfect venue to simply be together.

After parking near York Gate, the first obstacle to confront them was a lack of a nearby dropped kerb. Having made the unpleasant trek in the busy road to find it, Richard found himself staring at a pile of rubble and workers' barriers. The hole they had made was a bottomless pit, sucking in his plans and hopes, laughing at him.

'Fuck. This is fucking pathetic. Why can't we fucking well go about our lives like every other fuck? Why?'

'Oh Rich, I know. It's the usual shit, and you know that. No one really cares what it means to us. As in us being here, wanting to get into the park.' Charlie smiled encouragement. 'Let's find another kerb. We can't let fuck-ups like this ruin the rest of our day.'

Richard wanted to shimmy his fingers around her narrow face and warm up her high cheekbones.

'Yeah, you're right. If Yvonne walks with you in the road, we'll head for the next corner,' he muttered as heat shamed his face and a ratty voice in his head reminded him he was such a loser; that this sort of thing had to happen.

Grabbing the wheels of his chair, he pushed on, ignoring the whine. Charlie was with him, frustration at a buggered dropped kerb could not take that away.

They found a place in the park near a fountain and endless beds full of bright pink flowers that shook their worried heads as the squirrels rampaged through them. When Charlie told Yvonne it was okay for her to leave them, that she would call on the mobile when she was needed, Richard sank happily into the colluding sun.

'Oh, you trust me then,' he teased.

'Why, what plans did you have for me?' She gave him a grin that shone in her eyes. As she leant to one side, her breasts pushed together under the tight buttons of her jacket.

'Oh, that's my secret,' he played some more and felt spring bursting energy through his blood.

Background sounds of children giggling and dogs yapping overlapped with the sibilant murmurs of trees. The squirrels played games with them, following as they moved, darting closer for scraps of the bread roll Charlie had stashed in her bag at the bar for that purpose. Richard breathed in her happiness and surrendered to the comfortable meanders of their conversation.

What he already knew of Charlotte Tenerson was now supplemented with more. He could see the little bird girl with white bows in her brown hair, brought from Nottingham to London by her parents as a teenage indie kid. Into 'special' school that saw her bored and frustrated – later into mainstream school that saw her bullied. Then, settling into a self she liked, her body unfurling like a flower, she bloomed through the fun of university. She worked in the field of disability access, but was not doing much at the moment. There was also the usual grind of hospitals and doctors, which she admitted she copped out from as much as possible.

The one blushing gap in these exchanges was on relationships. Richard picked at the wood on the bench he sat alongside in his wheelchair. He had not been forthcoming either, what could he expect? It remained a hollow between them, his words to know more coming to his mouth as crunchy as last year's dry leaves, now creaking under the scratching paws of the indefatigable squirrels.

He remembered to tell her about Mary from Albania, and relished her enjoyment and thanks as she discreetly took the drugs from his pocket and paid him immediately. He looked at his watch and knew the evening was looming to cheat him out of much more time with her.

'That'll keep me going for a day two,' she laughed, but he caught a hint of sadness trailing with her into the sinking sun.

They sat near the bench forming an accidental tableau. Wheelchairs positioned in opposite directions, they almost faced each other, side by side, his larger wheels against the smaller apparatus of her power-chair.

'Charlie, we'll have to go soon.' His head felt dizzy with the afternoon as the faltering sun made uneven shadows across the tidy flowerbeds. The journey to her flat in East London would take a while, and he remembered he'd left the last night's dinner-plates unwashed and gathering spores on the drainer.

'Rich, it's been great here today. We should do it again, somewhere else.' She looked down at her fingers curling in her lap on the hugging denim skirt.

Richard smiled. She had asked him out, hadn't she?

'We can do this anytime you're up for it. No problem.'

'Rich… I'm not such a perfect person, really. Just… take me as I am and we'll do fine.'

'And? It sounds like there's more to come, Charlie,' he said, wanting to the point of agony to scoop her close.

'Would you take me home? Drop me off, I mean.' She caught his eyes then flew her gaze away into the shadows. Richard sighed. A no-entry sign fell in front of her as dark as the growing bands dragging colour from the park.

'I'll drop you off, yes of course I will. I'm not leaving you here, am I?' he whispered. He felt as if Charlie had shed a skin – Charlie, with *those* breasts – was now an uncertain fragile creature, as she sat beside him in the park.

'Well, I'm ready when you are. The journey's a bit of a bummer, isn't it?' Charlie said, and he could see her mood hugging itself.

'I'll manage. We'll pick up Yvonne on the way out and off we'll go.'

She didn't move but stared at the grass, now black with the stain of evening. Richard could not bear to see her sharp little face with its cheekbones, eyelids made to kiss, fallen into sadness. He found his hands reaching forward.

'I'm going to kiss you goodbye first.' He said it and did it, assisting her to lean towards him, her face brightened with questions, soft under his lips in a moment that emptied the park of shadow and rushed the sap of the trees into his belly, and his heart.

'You're a sly one, aren't you?' She grinned at him. 'Is that what you brought me here for?'

He saw her face, as calm as a cat, and bravery flowed.

'That and other things maybe. But I don't think the park authorities would approve.'

'Cheeky.'

'How cheeky do you want me to get?' He put his hand over hers as the shadows enclosed them.

'What I want is you to drop me off home.' Charlie laughed, but didn't push his hand away.

They drove into snarls of traffic but the world was a glitz of magic and promise, every slow car a sign of approval, every red traffic light a means to keep them together. She flirted with him now and he felt the stab of his desire lift, as he hooted at black cabs and timorous outcasts lost in their cars in the central London gridlock.

*

Dropping Charlie at her Hackney flat, Richard quivered. He wanted to park the Vito, flip into his chair and share a goodbye kiss. But holding himself back, he left with a quick wave, and shot out along the A12 link road to his pale beige palace in Dagenham. The plates, decorated with a bas-relief of food, were flung into soak, and he made it into bed by 12.10.

The night felt cold, despite the promise of the warm daytime sun, yet Richard felt heat roll like illness inside him. Charlie had promised to ring, and he knew most women kept those promises – what else could he do but wait? The flat semi-darkness of his room, with the disjointed drone of the A13 nearby, compelled a buzzing doubt into his thoughts. When – if – she rang, what next? He wondered, and then wondered for over an hour, complicating himself into intricate knots of possible disappointment.

Desire was itching, a demanding demon that burnt a void. He pulled himself to a position where he could touch his cock. He couldn't always come by simply rubbing himself, but it was good to feel it there in his hand, to always grin in memory at the notions doctors and family had about his ability to function sexually. Okay, so it wasn't always straightforward, his cock didn't always behave – but it was many years back to the fretting puberty, since there had been any serious issues about doing *It*, his masculinity, his ability to *perform*.

Inevitably, he thought of the last time. With Rachael, the bitch. He would not feel guilty for that, she *was* a bitch and perhaps he had been a complete dickhead. He wasn't claiming total innocence in their break-up, but he knew, in the end, they had wanted different things. Rachael, with a tight blonde bob, missus-tight-arse-right-on, with her career in teaching. She had been a bright, shiny prize. He had loved her, and he clung to that belief as he kept his hand on his penis.

They were good in bed, that couldn't be denied. She had more mobility than he had, used to walk on crutches, and would ease herself backwards on his lap, down to enclose his cock as he held her around the waist. If his tackle wouldn't go for that, sometimes she would edge onto a table, lift her legs over his shoulders and he would dive for the luscious pearl between the light flush of her pudenda, sinking into the delirium of her intense pleasure that then glutted him with his own.

His hunger grew and he found memory staggering helplessly to Kitty. Kitty, such a joke name for a prostitute. He had told her that, too. Why didn't she just call herself pussy? A big woman from Bristol, she had laughed, settled the money business, and quickly rode him to exhaustion. He'd paid for Kitty three times now and it always left his desire steamrollered on a rough road of guilt and prickly motives.

It was Alan, a casual mate who hung out with them all sometimes, who recommended the brisk blonde-haired woman. A big guy of thirty, Alan did the thing, it seemed to Richard, with efficiency and clean respect. With his negligible mobility, he declared he had a right to answer that itch by paying.

'I'm not saying I won't ever have a relationship in the usual sense, or any of that shit,' he told Rich in his meticulous, educated voice. 'But that'll be a different issue. If she's disabled one way or another, we'll need a military approach to complete the operation, as it were. But with Kitty, I get that urge and I need it sorted. I only do it when I can afford to pay and I always follow her rules.'

Richard wished he could file his feelings into these pragmatic categories with brick-wall boundaries, sealed off with signs on doors that said *don't think about this too much*. Kitty didn't seem oppressed and immediately after her business was complete, a weight would lift from him until the guilt loaded in its place.

He had heard Mel say to Alan, 'I'm totally there with your dilemma, Al. We're human beings who have a right to fuck. But would you be happy if your sister – or mother – made little Kitty visits to other disabled guys? I'm not saying I'm against you having sex, but this is a messy issue.' Alan had agreed wholeheartedly and no one had known what else to say, but Richard knew that Kitty's visits to Alan remained regular – although he hoped, shamefully, no one knew about her calling on him.

Richard paused from stroking his cock and Charlie flushed into his mind. Not only was there the axe of this uncomfortable transgression hovering by his neck, but he realised that to want Charlie was one thing, but now, the storm inside him stirred with speculation. How would they do it, if he dared to think that maybe they would? It was a poor consolation to remember that with Rachael it had taken a little while;

that in the beginning there had been the compulsory aphrodisiac of play, exploration and even drugs. He realised he didn't know the full definitions of Charlie's mobility. It just wasn't the thing to ask. Medical details were seldom necessary and Richard knew that most of his disabled friends never discussed it. This was as it should be and he had no urge to repeat the tedium of answering – or diverting – ghoulish questions as to what was 'wrong' with him. In the supermarket, at work, even from his cleaner with her black startled eyebrows that rose like prurient question marks, 'You-a hurt your-a legs bad darlink?'

I'm too fucking horny for the luscious Charlie Tenerson, that's what's wrong with me, he wanted to yell at them all and jaunt his crotch at the crowds.

A loud car squealing down the road drove off with his lechery and he let go of his cock. Moving his legs to a comfortable position, he closed his eyes, resolute for sleep and the new day that would, he hoped, begin the forward journey of Richard and Charlie.

*

Immersed in fixing a stubborn computer all day, Richard arrived home from work, dismissed his junk mail and prepared a stir-fry.

Charlie was on his mind, nestling in some warm part of himself, but when the phone rang, he still swore and crashed the wok into the sink, vegetables yelping up in colourful dismay.

Charlie's voice glided into his ear and he stared at the pale beige wall to concentrate. The next day at seven, could he make it? Of course he could, he'd careen through work, pause for a spruce up, and be there sharp. When he went back to the sink, his wok had sunk into the dirty dishwater, the vegetables poking up from the grey scum like exotic drowning worms.

He grinned, pulled the plug out and started dinner from scratch.

*

Charlie's flat was along a cul-de-sac on the corner of a small 1930s block. He parked the Vito and flipped out into his wheelchair as quickly as he could manage. Ignoring the rush in his ears, he skimmed to the front door. It opened before he buzzed the intercom.

'Hello Rich, how are you?'

'Better now I'm here,' he mumbled shyly, but he meant it. 'And you?'

'Boring day. I'm all over the place at the moment. A bit weary I suppose. Too much substance abuse, perhaps.'

They laughed together as she moved back to let him into the flat. He detected the light fresh smell of an oil burner and the pebble-blue carpet swayed like a calming sea beneath his wheels. Her lounge flickered with tall white candles, matched with a single white lily in a dark blue vase.

'Dinner won't be long. Do you fancy a glass of wine first?'

'That'd be great, cool,' he said, letting the words saunter from his mouth.

They drank two glasses together, chatting about the bar and the park. Yvonne came in and they went to the kitchen for the meal, where more candles glowed –

and some sexy tracks by Portishead played in the background. Soon, preliminaries of serving attended to, the personal assistant retired and they were alone.

'I feel spoiled by this. A candlelit dinner,' he smiled and drank more wine. They ate together, speaking with full, enthusiastic mouths. His chest tightened ashe took in her blue top that hung around the thrust of her breasts. Her skirt was blue with tempting silver buttons along the front. After the meal, they sat closer to each other, but he could not quite dare to touch her.

'Well, not everyone gets this treatment, so you must be getting the message. Are you?' Her voice floated in the haze of the light. 'I like you a lot, Rich. But I have to tell you some things first. About me. Me and Jeff.'

His heart ripped from his chest, smacked him, and punched back through his ribs. He couldn't breathe.

'What about you, and Jeff?'

'The obvious, silly. We had a, well, call it a fling, not long ago. It ended up being a bit messy. I don't know if we really ended it, as we should have. It wasn't exactly a great romance.'

Richard froze and saw Charlie jouncing on Jeff's firm thighs, the brakes on his sporty wheelchair firmly clicked, her breasts muffling his face. He choked to recall Jeff's lewd comments about Charlie's *nice tits* – but punching him would have to come later – for now only the blue vase on Charlie's table shook nervous and nearby as a plausible victim.

'And?' Somewhere, a plaintive voice coaxed him not to be stupid.

'I feel a bit scared, that's all. About things moving too quickly. Don't sound so shocked, please.'

Silence screeched loudly between them.

'Well, what next? Is that it? You go off in a bloke-ish huff?' Exasperation cooled the edge of her voice.

Richard could still see Jeff groaning upwards into the peachiness that Charlie's slender body promised. A great hammer smacked in his chest.

'No, no. I won't do that.' His words felt like loose chains that wouldn't link together. He knew he would stay, and would battle the childish green-eyed enemy, get over the outrage of Charlie daring to have a life, to have a past that hadn't featured him.

'So, you don't see Jeff now then?'

'No. It was a casual thing in a way. Not that I'm easy about sex, don't get that idea. We fancied each other. I know, Rich, that you're not a saint on these matters. Anyway, why should it concern you so much? One kiss and I'm yours!'

'I'm sorry. You know I'm keen, Charlie. Keen on us.'

'Yes, I do know.' Her voice lapsed to a sigh, full of promises that dissolved his jealousy.

'Let's just forget about it then? Enjoy tonight?' His voice was cautious and he blinked his eyes, staring at the lily.

'If I say, "here Kitty-Kitty", does it help?' Charlie said, suddenly.

Richard found himself jabbering and cold.

Charlotte persisted. 'You can do that and it's okay, while it's not if I have a fling with Jeff?'

She had moved closer now and he saw her thin hand lifting towards him. Portishead oozed a grinding track.

'Shall we call it quits? And you should give me a proper kiss.'

He obeyed, listening to something other than cry-baby envy.

Everything sparkled in Charlie's home and he leant towards her, straining in his chair to get him arms around her. Things were going to change.

Their mouths joined freely, fierce with hope.

Thunder Lightning Days

Every week you could see them. Cripples poking about the market and shopping mall, pushed in wheelchairs by carers with hard faces, some let loose in power chairs or big scooters that scythed through the thick knots in the crowd. There would be strings of them on foot, made to hold hands and follow a stern helper. Every other person who pushed by would mutter *retards*.

Fran froze and held back every time she saw a disabled person. So what if she used a wheelchair? She was different, and not part of some embarrassing *special needs* group shoved out for its weekly airing with the normal people.

Kelly was there, in her black baggy clothes and thick brown boots, always trying to catch Fran's eye. Fran glanced at her from behind a make-up bag but said nothing. They had been close friends once, attending Special School together, picked up by the same bus for years. The bus that had bitchy Bernie, the driver's assistant, who they enjoyed hating together as she flung them into their seats like little rag dolls. Bernie, with envied shining hair, touching herself all the time in front of overweight Baldy Georgie who drove the horrible, rough bus.

The nervous memories flexed a smile on Fran's face, but she shovelled most of that time away as something not worth keeping, sharp with her mother's shame that she had gone to a school for *The Physically and Mentally Handicapped*. No time wasted in getting her away from it on the stroke of her 16th birthday; away from the *abnormals*, as her mother called her schoolmates.

If she was honest, Fran admitted she missed Kelly. They tried to keep some contact, but Kelly's parents had been much older than Fran's, and a few years after those school days, Kelly was assessed and organised into the place she had now lived in for twelve years. A drab sprawl of uniform red-brick boxes with a large square centre that housed an activities block. It was called Gerrard Place, and Fran feared it. Her mother said it had *cripple* written all over it, and, thank goodness, her Fran would never need such a thing.

*

It was a clear autumn day and the crisp fallen leaves made little whirlwinds with rubbish from the market. Fran wore a black cape trimmed with a subtle fur edging. Her small Russian hat matched it and her boots were black and shiny. Her hair was a ringleted brown-black, her blue eyes delicately accentuated with a hint of make-up.

She didn't shop with a carer, it was important to make an effort, and she wanted to remind the world she was normal and not to be associated with those happy to be screaming their handicap all down the market.

When she went into The Body Shop she chilled away the approaching shop assistant with a smile of icicles.

'No thank you, I'm fine. I can manage.' Fran didn't mean to be unfriendly, but somehow the words were often out and on the attack before she knew it. The startled assistant was not the enemy. She knew that, really, but her mother had trained her, and the training was thorough and ongoing. She wouldn't accept her daughter was a cripple, like a *spastic* or something. If Mum had waged that war for all those years, and the battle against giving into *it,* then Fran wasn't about to surrender, either.

She edged her wheelchair slowly through the shop, not picking up anything. In reality, she couldn't manage that alone but it didn't matter. Her mother would buy them later when she had chosen what she wanted.

As she passed by the check-out, she caught the attention of a young man with beautiful almond eyes and delicate brown skin. Her chest constricted and she tried a smile that didn't come garlanded with frost.

'Can I help at all?' His gaze was on her. Just her. Her stomach churned.

A herd of noisy young women giggled into the shop. His focus flipped.

'Hey, Lee, you going out with Jayden later?' A girl with fair floppy hair leant across the counter, her bust firm and perfect in a tight denim jacket.

Fran slipped to invisible. When she heard one of them hiss and laugh *mind the spaz* she couldn't help the tears threatening from under her soft lids.

Mum told her to be proud, always. Move away and don't show emotion.

She was *better* than them, and the tawdry handicapped lot who kept coming to the market these days. Her mother said so.

But when Fran sat alone in her pink bedroom, surrounded by a large teddy army, she would cry and know that she was useless and unloved.

Not at all sexy, like those girls in the shop.

Everyone knew the neighbours called her mother *that bloody Beryl Lane*. They would all pull suffering faces if she caught them for a little chat about her efforts with her Franny, and how well Franny was doing. They had heard it before and knew they would hear it again.

Beryl Lane never talked to Fran about anything much other than to obsess about her medical issues, and to know if she was comfortable. Sex – and love – was never up for discussion.

Many years before, Fran asked her mother about a dream she had had in which someone was touching her between her legs. She woke up feeling warm and peculiar, if half-afraid.

The week following this dream was an explosion of severe washing routines in the shower, trips to the doctor and her mother's face buttoning in, closing the shutters. Her eyes, threatening tears when she looked at Fran.

Eventually her mother said, 'It's all right, love. We know now from the doctor for definite. You really can't feel anything, down *there*. All that business won't really have to trouble you.'

Fran still had similar dreams, now and then. With the soft touching came whispers and unnerving visions of an unknown *thing* pushing through her pallid bedroom curtains. She would still wonder about this 'not feeling' and was sure she could experience sensations in a way that she could never explain to her mother, and definitely not a doctor. TV, books and glossy girls' magazines had told her long ago about sex and babies, and all the curious fussing people expressed about love. She felt it would not concern her and if she ever wondered about it, her mother was there to iron out any shabby creases of doubt.

As Fran got older, even the tiny little tiffs about what clothes she should wear became bitter competitions with Mum. How could she say what she truly felt when it required so much effort of care and tact?

Once she had longed to have a dress that clung around her bust at the top with a lovely flowing skirt falling below. Fran wore a brace high around her torso, and she – and her mother – knew it was essential to hide it. But why should she hide her bust, too?

So many men are perverts. That was a favourite cheap gift from her mother's neat parcels of answers. *You can't fend for yourself. Don't advertise your body, Frances, it's not nice, especially in your situation.*

Fran knew if she could only resist, just once, to say, no, I don't believe you, Mum. You can't be right about everything. So far, after 33 years of living with her mother, she had not yet managed it.

*

Apart from the enjoyment of window shopping, Fran especially loved browsing the internet for friends. Bloody Beryl Lane approved and felt it broadened her poor daughter's horizons, allowing her some nice little friends, while not requiring physical effort – or contact – on either side.

Fran found much pleasure from writing long letters to people all over the world. But the rule was never to admit something was wrong with you. Her mother was strict on this point.

'That sort of thing puts people off,' Beryl would say in her low voice, a straight, slashed mouth hanging open. 'There are lots of other things you can tell them. You have a pretty enough face, you have nice clothes, you read a bit.'

Fran would smile and roll her eyes at the teddy bears. She was sure Barbie-May from Colorado would love that. Barbie-May liked knitting baby blankets and making toys from old socks. Fran wrote to her mainly because she had put in her entry in the directory that she never went out much because of a 'health problem'. She sent Fran a photo via email and it turned out that Barbie-May was fat. Very fat. Fran flushed with unkind thoughts that Barbie-May was totally gross-out ugly and probably didn't have any friends. To resist telling her she had her own *problems,* was really easy.

There was Rayn from Australia, one of only two men she wrote to. Rayn, she loved his daft name. Sitting in front of the screen, her cheeks would tingle and her pulse flitter from knowing he was a secret from her mother.

Ignoring the little hammocks of teddies arranged in orders of colour and size on each of the four pastel pink walls, she would eagerly check her email every evening while her mother watched the soaps.

Rayn was a torrent of humour, hooting and male into her small frilly bedroom. His questions were endless and could be tricky. Has she seen Buckingham Palace? No? Has she seen The Tower of London? Not ever? What had she seen at the cinema lately? Nothing? What colour were her eyes? Did she have a boyfriend?

Why was she so bloody secretive?

Fran evaded his questions with her own about Australia, which would keep him happy for awhile. Her other online pals were also good topics. Barbie-May, she is so gross, ha-ha, she told him, relishing each retold detail of Barbie's stupid knitting, the silly toys – and impossible fatness.

His reply was a bullet shattering through the screen. 'Are you really so horrible and tactless?' he said. 'I might have a weight issue too, y'know! We've never swapped photos, after all.'

The bold remarks stabbed through her nightmares for weeks. Worse still was his silence, with no email for over a fortnight.

When it all picked up again, he never referred to her as horrible and tactless but Fran knew things had changed. She struggled with the growing sense that she couldn't compete with him, jumping and vigorous, out in the world, keen to hear about *life in London,* which he had never been to yet.

But she didn't know much about life in London either, despite always living there. There was mostly her mother, a long woman with ruffled big brown hair who wore slacks and poorly matching blouses. All they did was live together and go to hospitals. Apart from the market and mall every week, Fran couldn't remember any real visit to anywhere or anything – only to the homes of aunties and uncles, and a few cousins on rare occasions.

Her father, Mr Fred Lane, had scampered off with a generous brunette from the Co-Op when his daughter was three – as a direct result, the family declared, of Fran's *problems.* He was now the resident demon in the home, the root of all their woes, and bloody Beryl Lane only kept his name to polish her badge of respectability.

Rayn made Fran conscious that so much of her life seemed to belong to her mother. She told herself it was okay, mum was the best and she loved her of course, in a way that most people had forgotten to love their mums.

Yet Rayn pushed something into the happy nest, and into Fran. A thin wedge of curiosity for something her mother could not give.

*

The day for the market shouted through her curtains with great whoops of thunder and showy blasts of lightning. Fran's mother helped her out of bed, into the bathroom on the hoist. Into the shower, then scrub-scrub-scrub with minute attention.

'Not sure you should go to the market today. Franny, love, listen to that weather.'

'Mum, I won't melt away, will I?' Fran loved the market and mall, even with the others, the embarrassing handicapped.

'No, you might get cold. If you do want to go, I'll have to catch up on housework later and come with you.'

'Mum, no. Really, I'll be okay.'

Fran tried to sound assertive but it was impossible as her mother lifted her left breast and meticulously soaped it.

Fran suddenly rushed with a sensation of imagining the mouth of the gorgeous shop assistant pinching his lips around her nipple. A gentle whisper flowered over her skin. Fran closed entry to the thought quickly, afraid as her mother continued scrubbing her back.

The two piddly hours she spent at the market on her own was her only gasp of freedom all week. If her mother came she would be impossible, constantly fussing. Straightening Fran's hat, fidgeting her hair, sometimes even getting a tissue out to clean her face.

The thunder shook the sky in a glory of noise and rain fell like spew from black-hearted clouds.

'I'll order the special cab then, we'll have fun together Franny.'

Hearing the pet-name she hated – it sounded like *fanny* for god's sake – Fran knew the battle was over. She let her mother move and prepare her in a stream of banal chatter, and flopped to become a large mute doll, played with by a contented child.

*

At the market, Fran saw that the weather had not discouraged the others, the handicapped lot, and she admitted to being pleased. It would annoy her mother. Why shouldn't they – all of them – be able to come out in the bloody rain if they wanted to?

Stopping in the food section at the mall for lunch, Fran watched with her stern blue eyes as Kelly appeared in a new powered chair, moving closer to their table with a tall dark woman at her side.

Kelly looked different and Fran couldn't work out why. She had on her black things and her hair stuck up in a strange fern-like frond.

Kelly was grinning. 'Hello, Fran you old bag. Can we sit here too?'

'Yes, of course.' Fran tried to smile back. It would disgruntle Mum and might send her off for a while. Sitting with Kelly was okay as long as none of the others appeared.

'This is Vicky, my personal assistant.' Kelly gestured to the young woman then looked intently at Fran. 'We've known each other since we were kids, haven't we Fran?'

'Yeah, we have,' Fran mumbled, scanning the crowds by the counter for her mother.

'You should sort yourself out and get a PA too you know,' Kelly continued as she watched Fran's eyes. 'I see you're still joined at the hip with your darling mama.'

'What's wrong with my mother?' Fran flared. That had always been Kelly's problem. She liked to think she was better than everyone else was.

'Ooo, sorry,' she teased gently. 'Pressed a button there, didn't I?'

Fran fell silent and studied the pattern contained inside the glass-top tables and realised they were adverts. One was for cheap air flights to Australia.

'Anyhow, I'm not here to pick an argument with you. I'm moving, yeah. Moving. Don't look like a startled bunny,' Kelly chuckled and Fran saw now that her black clothes consisted of smart jogs and a sharp designer label shirt. And did she have red highlights in her hair?

'Where to? When? How on earth did you sort it all out?'

'Hello, Kelly Anne Smith.' Fran's mother appeared looking sulky in the effort to pull politeness over her plain, long face.

Fran squirmed, torn between Kelly's news and shame at her mother. Why did she say it like that? Kelly wasn't five years old!

She knew her mother would be disturbed that it looked like a cripples' gathering at their table. Something wriggled, a tiny defiant snake winding its way through the hard rock of so much obedience. She wanted to hear Kelly's incredible news, she did, and she would admit to envy.

'I've wanted to move for years,' Kelly continued. 'I hate that sheltered housing place and always have, that's the joke of it. Ghetto of rabbit hutches. I've got a neat little flat in Leytonstone, on a small estate. Two bedrooms, one for me, the other for PAs.'

'What's a PA, Kelly-Anne Smith?'

Fran heard the sharpened edge to her mother's voice and tensed.

'This is a PA.' Kelly laughed and turned her eyes to Vicky, who said a polite hello. 'The Social Services gave me money to pay their wages, after a bit of a fight. But it means I choose the type of person I want, Fran. And I can do pretty much what I like. Get up late, go out, go to bed late. Eat dinner at eleven, breakfast at two. Imagine that!'

Kelly laughed again and Fran found herself giggling. There was the rigid drill in their house and her mother didn't believe in slackening it.

'Are you trained, dear?' Beryl Lane looked at Vicky, doubt in her jet eyes as she took in the dreadlocks and pierced eyebrow.

'I don't need them to be trained, really,' Kelly spoke up quickly. 'Vicky is my arms and legs, if you like. I train her. Train her how I want.'

'Well, my little Franny doesn't really need strangers to help her. She's got me, haven't you love? And mums come free!'

Silence unfolded at the end of her exclamation.

'Yeah, not forever though.' Kelly pushed aside the hush softly.

'I'm not retiring from being there for my Frances, just yet. I'm fit as a fiddle, me,' bloody Beryl Lane snapped, her eyes rolling from Kelly to Fran.

Fran knew Kelly hadn't meant it like that. Her mother would die, one day. Of course she would.

It was something she thought of all the time. But her mother's control was as sure and unfailing as the tight, ancient girdle thing she wore. She wasn't going anywhere for years and years, she stated, especially when ironing. And anyhow, then Auntie Rose was there to take charge, it was all organised. Fran wanted to point out that Auntie Rose didn't even visit that much and Mum wasn't keen on her younger sister. But to challenge was to rip the veil of self-sacrifice her mother wore so well and, as always, Fran ended up saying nothing.

'Anyhow, look, Fran, I don't know whether you'll be able to make it, but I'm having a flat warming party when I'm settled,' Kelly said. 'You've got to come. Please. I know we've lost touch a bit over the years, but it'd be lovely to see you, in my own flat.'

'I'd love to.' Fran heard the words and smiled at them, pleased they had escaped and avoiding her mother's glare.

'She'll try and make it. Is it in the afternoon?' Her mother spoke in abrupt doubtful statements.

'Not sure. I'd like it to be an evening thing really. We can all stay up late, get a little bit boozy,' Kelly laughed, then turned her face in quick realisation. They both stared at Beryl Lane and pressed back into their chairs, braced for the reaction.

'Boozy? I don't think so, Kelly Anne Smith. We don't drink and Frances goes to bed at 9.30pm. That's right, isn't it, love?'

Fran drew in a long slow breath, creating a pause. She sipped wine at Christmas parties with the family and the time for bed was a commandment hacked from the slab of her mother's personal bible of rules.

'I'm sure I could come for a little while at the beginning,' she said, holding her mother's stare.

Lightning gashed the sky above them, shrieking white through the hexagonal roof of the mall. Thunder belched rain that rattled nails on the glass.

'We must get going now, Frances.' Beryl Lane stood up, as though the noise was a signal, and gathered their bags in a movement that thrust away further discussion.

'I'll give you a ring, maybe?' Kelly asked. 'We shouldn't lose touch totally, Fran. After all the time we've known each other.'

'Okay, yeah, I'd like that,' Fran found her voice was soft and hopeful, coming from regions that felt rusty. 'What about email?'

'Yes, definitely. I'll ring first and we'll swap addresses.'

'I would if I were you,' Beryl Lane interjected. 'Our cab will be waiting. Time to go.'

Fran left as the storm raged and she felt as though it shook inside her.

'Don't get soaked,' Kelly called out, and suddenly Fran wanted to cry.

*

Fran didn't go to Kelly's flat-warming, which was several weeks later. Her mother said that actually she wasn't used to being alone in the evenings and it wasn't much to ask of Franny, after everything.

Picking at, and then refusing the consolation prize her mother offered of her favourite dinner, Fran quickly shut herself in with the computer screen, suffocated by the rows of teddy bears.

As she tapped the keyboard to go online, she felt empty with the weight of disappointment but as the messages flipped into her Inbox, they lessened her curiosity about Kelly's party, her flat, her PA and friends.

Barbie-May had written to say she'd started on a kitten made from her sister's green socks. Rayn told her it was getting hotter and there were a lot of spiders about, the ones that hid in the toilet. He wished he could show her Christmas on an Aussie beach. Suddenly she heard her mother's voice in her head, 'Hello, Rayn Michael Mellings.' Fran giggled, saw him bouncing beside her on the pretty pink bed in his silly hat with corks, her mother aghast in the doorway.

There was also one from her *other* male friend, Greg. She stared at it and read it several times. A dizzy feeling made hot spirals on her cheeks. She read it again, holding her breath.

Fran, so I know your so-called secret. I don't care. Everything will be okay with me, Fran. I bet now you want to be fucked senseless by me don't you? Well, Baby, I wanna spunk over those juicy little scars on your luscious crippled body. We're both adults. You could say this is my special thing. But don't let those right-on types call me a pervert and put me down. I want to worship you baby, head to toe. Write soon, Fran. I kind of guessed things would go this way. I am yours and waiting for you. I know you live in London, that's not difficult for me to get to. I hope we can meet up soon. Hot Love from your Greg x

It was a chilly night with only a few fireworks warming up the sky. She curled like a rag wrung tightly at Greg's outpouring and read the email repeatedly. He had wheedled into her mind, laid a safe path of rose petals with happy tales of his disabled friends. Of his first wife, who had been disabled, and damn sexy with it, in her leather and steel callipers.

The strands of her past combined suddenly to pose many possibilities.

Maybe Greg had fallen in love with her? She waltzed the idea around her head, grinned at her teddies, their stiff arms raised in sneering celebration.

He was the one, her pal in Oxford on a site called Special Wheelchair Friends, who had been trusted, the one who she had chosen as worthy enough to defy her mother's words. The mention of the disabled wife surely made him safe and real. In her third email she had said yes, I have *problems* too. Yes, what a coincidence, I wear a brace.

It had grown from there as she welcomed his interest, his easy questions about her body. Lots about her body, which made her hot and curious, bringing back the warmth between her legs.

She typed: *Greg I don't know what to say right now, but I think maybe we should meet up soon.*

While the fantasy carried her away, she clicked send. She felt grown up, adult, a feeling very new.

A firework ruptured the dream and she realised it was almost 9.30. She closed her email and decided that Kelly was really the only person who she could possibly share this with.

Tomorrow would be a good day to do it, with the apology she had to make for not managing to get to the party. Since meeting up in the mall they had emailed every day and Fran wondered why they had drifted apart so much before, when they got on so well.

During the next day, somehow she never got around to Kelly, and had no time to check out Greg's mail. Her mother had a cold and insisted that Fran sit with her in the front room, making Christmas present lists and deciding how much money they could spend.

The day after that was the market with fresh jolly sunshine putting colour into the grey streets. Fran managed to ask for help with buying things and allowed herself to wonder more about Greg. Her face glowed with the novelty and she made a promise to herself that Kelly had to be told later that day. Maybe Kelly would know what he meant by saying *you could say this is my special thing.*

When the cab dropped her off at home, the first thing she saw was Auntie Rose's car. Next to it, an ambulance outside their flat, its doors ominous arms flung open wide.

*

Part of Fran was missing, the umbilical cut was savage and unforgivable. She lay on her bed, holding a pink teddy against her face but the pale rose curtains couldn't disguise the heavy sky now lurching into winter. Her eyes were bruised from crying and her head was one throb of too much thinking.

A neighbour who had spotted the open door of the flat had found bloody Beryl Lane – sprawled in the hallway, her head on the fluffy slippers by the phone table, as if nestling down like a cat. The neighbour insisted she looked peaceful. The doctor declared it a heart attack and there was an immediate whispering fire burning through their street that it wasn't a surprise after all she did for that bloody daughter of hers, who should have been in a care home years ago.

Fran huddled in her bed, now a murderer.

Auntie Rose was a thin woman, all spindly limbs and eyes of cold blue, just like Fran's. For five weeks she stayed at the flat with Fran, struggling with the drill. Swiftly it became a frayed and tattered routine, crumpled by their mutual unfamiliarity.

'My poor big sister,' Rose would sigh as they fought like soldiers to storm the wet and dangerous barricade the shower had become. 'I didn't quite realise you couldn't do all this yourself, and the toilet stuff.'

Fran didn't say much. Her mouth had become a flapping thing, trembling only when her eyes howled with new tears. It seemed as if her brain made remote notes on what was happening, like an internal secretary filing them for later; the horror of the funeral, the sense of being flung into a pit to sink down into the darkness.

Yet, at last, a morning came when grief hardened into a dull fear for the future.

In her bedroom washing piled up in the corner and the teddies waved their arms under the light settling dust. Her PC sat mute in rejection on her desk, a sullen inanimate object waiting for her interest to bring it to life.

Auntie Rose's cooking was atrocious and Fran could hardly believe how ignorant she was herself about the mysteries of roasting potatoes and getting a chicken to cook.

'I think we should have frozen and ready-cooked for now.' Auntie Rose served up the statement with red gelid meat and pitted golf-ball potatoes. 'I've never been one for this sort of fiddling about.'

Dark mutterings about Fran's imminent care assessment with a social worker crescendoed to a fixed appointment. Fran knew she had a social worker, her mother was always on the phone to them, sorting out something or other.

'I'm afraid things have to change for you, Fran.' Auntie Rose pistoned her arm along the ironing board, flattening the creases, and delicacy, in Fran's favourite blouse. 'There's much more involved in it all than I realised. I don't want to let you down, or go back on my word to poor Beryl, but there it is. I've done my best.'

She didn't iron out the rest of her statement with a smooth ending and Fran nibbled at her dry lips. Now her mother was always *poor* Beryl. Fran just couldn't think, it was best not to. She was still sinking into the darkness and there was no sign of hitting the bottom and finding the light.

*

The social worker's hair was cut like slabs of slate and she had a shiny, scrubbed red complexion. Her name was Ms. Parnell. Fran wondered why she didn't have make-up on.

There were endless forms from Ms. Parnell's brown briefcase, all breeding in its folds, as one form led to another. 'We realise losing your mother was a terrible shock,' Ms. Parnell said, in posh, meticulous lines.

Fran filled her with holes from the steel in her eyes. Confidence glistened easily on her ruddy face and Fran knew she had no idea what it was like to be called spaz and retard, and to have no one ever fancy you, shop assistants and all the rest – only some stranger on email called Greg, who she didn't quite understand.

'But we have to help you move on and decide.' Ms. Parnell's words came out well-formed. 'If you stay here we might be able to put in some sort of care. What do you think?'

Fran couldn't think. What would her mother do?

'She needs the lot. Toilet care and everything.' Auntie Rose, sitting nearby, stamped thin pointed feet on the carpet, over the stain she had made from leaving the hot iron on it.

'Yes, well, that is not disputed. The question is how Frances wants her care needs addressed. I feel, in the circumstances, that I should make my own recommendations and come back. In the meantime, we'll put in agency carers to cover the basics.'

There was a pause. Fran found herself caught on remembering Greg. Greg, waiting. Would he forgive her? Would he still be interested?

'Frances, would you consider staying at Gerrard Place, perhaps for a little while?' Ms. Parnell leant forward and grimaced with a rehearsed smile.

The descent was over, and as Fran suddenly shuddered back to life, she shook with visions of little red-brick boxes and cripples in circles knitting baby blankets and making toys from socks. She was there, in the middle, tangled in wool and weighed down by a carpet with a stain.

But Kelly was there, pulling the wool away, smiling and shaking her head, with copper red licks in her hair.

'No,' Fran said and meant it. 'Definitely not.'

She felt her mother somewhere, nodding a ghostly approval. But Fran pushed the presence away, and resisted the sadness that pulled her hair, that had tantrums in her head.

Kelly had rung her so many times since *poor* Beryl Lane had died. Fran had managed no more than a few words mangled by sobs. Now she realised. Kelly would know all about this, what to do. She would have words of advice about Greg too.

Kelly would help.

As soon as Ms. Parnell had packed away her rounded vowels and forms, Fran left Auntie Rose decimating the kitchen – for one more painful week – and went to her PC as something hinting at excitement stirred in her thoughts.

The neglected teddy bears shed invisible tears as they watched Fran Lane go online.

The Summer is Free

Part One

Linda sat in a wide high-ceilinged room at an old electric typewriter and for a while she stayed still, staring at a row of wicker baskets hung on a rusty metal frame.

She dreamed she was on a beach, the wind lifting her hair while in the distance a man approached. He was tall and walked with purpose, straight for her. Seagulls cried, the sun shone. The man was young and handsome, and he carried a single white rose. There was a soundtrack, The Smiths' *Reel Around the Fountain*, Morrissey's voice rich and full of a yearning she understood.

'We thought you were doing a letter, Linda Jones,' a shrill voice broke into her daydream.

'Yeah,' she said, and began to type the address, *beechwood unit for rehabilitation and physiotherapy*, before realising she should have capitalised each word.

'You know you're let off basket work to do typing,' the voice spoke up again. It belonged to tall crop-haired Miss Granston who ran the Occupational Therapy Unit at Beechwood. She nagged but she was okay, Linda didn't mind her. And being in OT was heaps better than school, which finished only six weeks ago after the tedium of an extra year they made her do.

The sun leapt through the one long window in the room. The summer itself tormented her, morning after morning, as the light came blasting into the four-bedded room where she slept. She felt she should be joining in somehow, but here, in the OT room, the summer made her feel imprisoned.

As the hospital radio's news bulletin came at four, everyone in the OT room left their tasks with relief, eager for the porters to take them back to their appropriate units.

Mark appeared first, the younger of the two porters, shirt sleeves rolled up. His brown hair was cut close, and his dark eyes flew to Linda's.

She smiled. Mark was nice.

'I'll save you till last,' he said, grinning back, as he manoeuvred away two old people in wheelchairs.

'Okay, but don't forget me.'

'Oh, as if,' he laughed and stroked her shoulder.

She felt happy. At least Mark was easy to talk to, wheeling her with deft hands from one section to another. Asking her how she was, was she bored, and, as he was unusually obsessed with socialism and politics, had she seen the dreadful news about Thatcher's latest nonsense?

It suddenly struck Linda that Mark was really quite tasty.

*

A few days later, he came to see her for no official reason. It was almost five, still over an hour until supper and the sunshine showed no sign of tiring. The older patients snored away in their section, the two nurses on duty huddled in the office. Linda was in the empty four-bedded room at the far end of the female unit, and struggled with the loneliness now her friends had been allowed home, but she could at least relish the privacy, relieved that no one noticed Mark.

She was encouraged to have a rest period during this time, after a day of exercise and occupational therapy. Before Mark appeared, she was fixated on the thought that the medical people kept promising she could go home soon, that they were working with the social worker to help her get a place at secretarial college by late September.

She didn't know what else to be but a secretary. Once she had hoped to be a vet but everyone at Beechwood told her that was out of the question with her disabilities.

Mark sat in her wheelchair beside the bed. She liked the way he always had something to say.

'We're doing a collection tomorrow, for the miners. You know they're on strike, I hope,' he said, flexing his fingers.

He was always fidgeting, drumming busy hands on everything. It made her laugh.

'I do watch the news. Hours and hours of it. More than you, probably.'

'If you give me 10p for the donation bucket I'll give you a sticker. You know it's a good cause. Those families have nothing. It's a scandal.'

'I hate Maggie Thatcher anyway,' Linda said. 'So you can have 20p.'

They chatted about a shared loathing of the Thatcher government. Linda changed position slowly and was now on her side with her head facing him. She felt awkward about sitting up, needing to swing her stiff legs hard to get herself upright. She was sure it looked really peculiar and decided to wait.

'Hey, Lin, do you know about the gazebo?' he asked suddenly, voice softening as he fiddled with the bottom of the t-shirt under his white porter's jacket.

'Gazebo?'

'You know, a little building. Like a summer house, kind of. There's one on the grounds, a really old thing. They call it the gazebo, anyhow. We should go and see it.'

She smiled, not sure how to answer. Mark grinned, eyebrows raised for a response.

'It can't be as boring as being stuck on this unit all the time,' she replied at last. 'Could we go tomorrow?'

'Yeah, why not? I finish at five. We'll sort out the details when I get you from OT.'

After supper and a tedious stretch of TV, Linda went to bed feeling restless. Her legs ached from the earlier exercise and the four-bedder was still and silent. Soon she followed an urge and masturbated gently, with some effort positioning a slim, quiet vibrator between her stiff legs. As soft pleasure rose up, she found she was thinking of Mark.

Did he fancy her? Was it stupid to think that? She felt that he liked her a lot but there were oodles of normal girls around the whole rehab centre. Doctors, nurses, cleaners, secretaries.

There was the problem with the staff who never wanted to accept the girls' thoughts about sex. They liked to hint to them that sex wouldn't be a part of their lives, because they were disabled, it just wasn't likely to happen. And you couldn't argue about it – the older girls all sensed that – because most of the staff were prudes who would clam up if you dared to try.

But she wanted to wonder about Mark. As she bit the sheet to stop the gasp of her orgasm being heard, she decided she didn't care. Whatever else, she would allow herself to have hungry thoughts.

*

The next day time seemed tied to a post, at great reluctance to move. She went to physiotherapy and through the drill. Push, pull, stretch, heave. This will improve posture, this will improve strength. With time, this will align the legs to look more normal. She looked at her legs, which were bent and patterned and different to most people's, and for once resisted the urge to argue with the physio that surely the exercises wouldn't do much for her after she had been chained to the same regime for several years.

As her stubbornly cramped hips were attacked with slings and procedures to make them move, she wanted to shout a question about sex – couldn't they at least make a useful suggestion about a way to do that?

Occupational therapy was a stream of prattle from the elderly people and sniping from a grouchy Miss Granston. Telling her to try harder and pay attention. Did she want to get into college or not? Didn't she realise she had to be better than everyone else to have a hope of getting a job?

As Linda had heard it all so many times before, she stayed silent and watched the clock. She dismissed the drowsy music on the radio but was pleased that the sun was waiting for her and Mark.

At four, the porters were back. Mark held the wheelchair as she made her way slowly on her crutches.

'You can be first today,' he said as they left the OT room. 'Are you still up for seeing the gazebo?'

'Of course I am,' she replied, hoping it wasn't too eagerly.

'We must be careful. That lot get so suspicious on your unit. Could you manage to meet me just outside, near the front car park? They'll let you out that far on your own, won't they?'

'Yes, but I'll only get away with an hour at most. You'd better not be an axe murderer or something though.'

'Now you know my secret,' he laughed. 'But it's my week off murdering young girls. No, really, I want to get you out of that dull unit. I promise I won't eat you or anything. Well, not all in one go.'

Linda giggled and blushed. 'Okay. It will be lovely to see the woods. I'm really looking forward to it.'

*

Once in her four-bedder, she busied herself with make-up. Nurse Jackie Scott brushed her hair, which was properly bleached blond, long, with a slight streak of pink on the fringe. Linda loved Jackie, who was only two years older than she was. Jackie could be trusted, but Linda wasn't ready to tell her about meeting Mark, just yet. It was only a spin in the woods, after all.

Unlike the other nurses, Jackie helped in a casual way without being bossy. She bent the rules and was the only one who was not shocked when the girls gossiped rudely about men they fancied.

The other nurse on duty was Staff Nurse Hampton, a big block of a woman who the girls decided was not quite human, and probably had sealed-up plastic private parts, like the Barbie dolls they all owned as kids.

'Why all this dressing up? You're going for a little sit in the sun, aren't you?' Jackie asked as she did up a silver chain around Linda's neck.

'I'm fed up moping. I want to make a bit of an effort.'

'You have lovely eyes, Lin, really. Those lashes,' Jackie sighed as they both looked at Linda's reflection in the mirror.

She wore a tight pink t-shirt over small but definite breasts. Jackie helped her into a short black skirt that revealed the unique shape of her knees but she didn't care. She looked good and felt good, which helped her to ignore the little nervous flips in her stomach.

'Be careful,' Jackie insisted as Linda wheeled herself slowly from the unit. 'I know you're up to something.'

Linda poked her tongue out and kept moving.

Outside it was warm with a happy breeze shimmying through the many trees which surrounded the complex of Beechwood. Mark appeared at one minute past five. The minute was the longest in Linda's day.

'You look great. I like that skirt,' he said, and took hold of her chair. She noticed his blue shirt was clean and nothing like the grey t-shirts he wore under his porter's jacket, and that he smelt of a delicious spicy aftershave.

His hands gripped the wheelchair with confidence, tilting her over bumps and edging along a small path that wound behind the main spread of buildings.

'I'm glad the sun is still out anyway,' he said as he spun her into the wood. 'It's great in here now. I think it's the best thing about this whole place. It's in a fabulous location.'

'Oh, a squirrel!' Linda gasped as the creature stared at them for a moment before bounding away. 'I love them, they're so cute.'

'I won't try and convince you they're vermin then,' he laughed. 'But they do cause problems. Saw the end of the red squirrel practically.'

'What a funny thing for a porter to know,' she said as they pushed on deeper into the dark jostling trees.

'I'm not intending to have a career in portering, Linda Jones,' he replied with mock scorn. 'I'm chucking in this wonderful line of employment very soon.'

Linda went cold. 'Not yet though. You stop me being bored.'

'I'm sure I can amuse you for several more months yet,' he reassured her and pushed her chair around a tight bend on the path, which by now was increasingly covered with foliage.

They came to a clearing. At the centre was a small stone building with a domed roof held up by several thin pillars. Under the roof, a stone bench circled around a larger central pillar that was decorated with ragged ribbons of ivy and bindweed. Jumbles of trees surrounded the open area, throwing down agitated shadows.

'What a weird little thing. Why do you think it's here?' Linda shivered. It smelt green and earthy as the heat of the sun baked the space.

'The land used to belong to some Lord Bloggs or other. You know, the scum aristocracy, ha-ha.' He pushed her chair so that she was beside the stone bench where he sat down. 'I think it's just a forgotten curiosity.'

He paused to reach into his pocket and pulled out a tin. Linda watched as he removed a scrawny looking roll-up. She realised it was a joint.

'Can I try some?' she asked, after he had taken a long drag.

'Have you done it before?' He looked at her doubtfully. 'It might react badly with your medications or something.'

'I do it every night, you bugger. Nurse Humpy-Hampton back there supplies it. Don't be silly. Let me try.'

She grinned and he held the joint out for her to take. Her small fingers strained to get hold of it. Without speaking, he pulled it back to ease it between her lips. Taking a tentative suck, the hot air rasped into her lungs. At once she felt harsh warmth fly through her blood and float into her head.

'Okay?' he smiled and took it back with curious eyes. 'Would you like to sit on this bench with me, Lin?'

'I can't get out of this chair easily. You've seen me wobbling about. You'll have to help me.' She didn't think it would be all that comfortable but decided she wanted to be closer to him. This was Mark, she felt okay, and he knew about her situation. It felt silly to be suddenly embarrassed.

The sunshine glimmered gold through the overlapping leaves. It was peaceful with the chatting birds and the distant sounds of occasional traffic.

She decided to be bold as Mark slipped his hands around her waist. She relished how he lifted her without effort, not causing her any pain. The bench was hard, putting a deep aching cold into her legs. She ignored it, looking at Mark's tanned arms and the dark hairs that ran along them. Heat rolled over her face as she looked at him, now right beside her.

When he put his hand on her leg, she was still surprised despite all her nighttime imaginings.

'What are you doing?'

'Touching your thigh, actually. Do you mind?' He stroked up and down, edging his fingers under the hem of her skirt, smiling.

'No. I'm just surprised.' In a flash of bravery she put her hand on his. 'Not what I expected.'

He moved so that his face was close and kissed her on the lips. With the softest movement, he eased the tip of his tongue inside her mouth. His arms wrapped around her. Her elbows protested and her back spasmed. She didn't care and flowed into the moment. He smelt good, he was warm and his arms felt safe. Energy flew up and she pushed her tongue towards his, tasting the herby cannabis in his warm mouth.

'Mmm, I enjoyed that.' Mark smiled as he drew back.

'Me too.' Linda felt as if the sun was in her belly, shooting light into her limbs. 'You know we'd scandalise Staff Nurse Humpy-Features.'

'I'd get the sack,' he grinned, stroking her hair. 'Don't look so worried. I don't care.'

'But I do,' she whispered. 'Even if I'm only number fifty on your list. You can't run away now.'

'Don't be silly. What do you think I am? I'm not that type.'

She chuckled. 'What type?'

'The type women go for, anyhow. Generally. I'm a titch smart-arse and beside that, I can't stand dummies. So I get too sarcastic too quickly, and then, bye-bye Mark.' He looked away into the woods but kept his arms around her.

'Maybe you'll think I'm a dummy. And I'm not exactly pin-up material am I?' She followed his gaze, watching the sun play along the treetops.

'You're not a dummy. You're gorgeous.' He put his fingers over her mouth as she started to protest. 'And clever. I can speak to you. Most of the bimbos around here don't know what a miner does, let alone that they're on strike!'

He moved his hand away and smirked.

Linda felt a tight churning in her chest. There were so many questions. But she wasn't sure if she wanted his answers yet, answers that might spoil things.

'Do you think we could come back tomorrow?' she said, leaning against him, loving his warmth.

'Of course we can. It's supposed to stay hot and sunny.' He tilted his head forward and whispered it into her hair, easing down to return to her lips.

Linda's frustration swam out to him as she returned his kiss. Her heart quickened and an ache began deep between her legs. He moved away from her mouth and kissed her ears. His hands rolled up her t-shirt, caressing over her breasts.

'Mark…,' she murmured, shocked at the speed of his intentions, yet hungry for him to continue. She found herself twisting to reach him, to stretch so that the restriction of movement in her hand could manage to find his lap. Below her fingers, she felt his erection.

His hand pressed on top of hers. She flinched at his strength.

'Oh god, did I hurt you? I'm sorry, Baby,' his voice was soft yet edgy. 'I'm in a state for you, I'm really sorry.'

'Shh. Stop apologising,' she whispered and kept her fingers on the stiff bulge in his jeans, flushed with courage. 'I have these, um, problems, Mark. You know you'll have to get used to that, don't you?'

'It doesn't bother me, Lin.' His serious eyes returned to hers. 'All this disabled stuff. I don't care. I want to spend time with you. As much as I can.'

'Let's enjoy ourselves then. We'll manage it somehow.' Even though her bottom felt numb from the bench, she wanted to sit beside him a bit longer.

The sinking sun revealed that time was passing too quickly, and for the remainder of the hour, they kissed and chatted, and kissed some more.

Mark was returning to university in London soon, after a year out, back to Zoology. As he talked, she realised how different their lives had been. His father was a solicitor, his mother a teacher. Besides portering, he surprised her by telling her how he had worked as a community service volunteer, assisting disabled people to live at home, doing the most personal tasks. She absorbed it carefully.

He didn't seem very upper-class, superior or posh. Yet he was not like any of the previous boys she had fancied. Nervy loud creatures, mostly from Beechwood's men's unit. With them, nothing had proceeded beyond holding hands, shy kisses and a clumsy grope.

She returned to the Unit reluctantly, dizzy with his masculine smell, now burning on her skin. When her supper was brought in, she tittered as she resisted Jackie's hissed questions.

In the seclusion of the four-bedder, the vibrator jolted her to orgasm as soon as she thought it was late, and safe enough. But it wasn't what she wanted. She wanted Mark and not just his mouth. As she remembered his hands on her body, she kept the vibrator on her clitoris and made the decision.

Somehow, despite the place, the risks, the staff, with their ridiculous ideas, and even the challenge of her unwieldy body, she would lose her virginity to Mark.

Part Two

When they next met up, Linda could see Mark was apprehensive.

'I don't want to hurt you, Lin,' he said. 'I don't know whether I should have kissed you like that yesterday.'

'Didn't you like it?' she asked, carefully hiding her dread. 'I know I did.'

'Oh silly. I fucking loved it,' he said and knelt beside her. 'I just can't imagine bringing you out here until it rains. And then what? I want to see you at other times too. Why should it have to be like this? All secret and in hiding. We're old enough to do what we want, aren't we?' He stood up and turned to the trees in a rough jerk. 'But, even then, is it right?'

'Do you ask this sort of thing every time you snog someone?' She held her breath. Surely this wasn't about her, after everything.

'No. It's not about anyone else. It's about you. And not what you're thinking.' He rushed the words, waving his arms. Then he was kneeling in front of her again, leaning over her, quickly on her mouth.

They blanked into each other. Linda eased him away, looking at his eyelashes, and the faint spots on his forehead. 'Let's just do what we can,' she said, wanting to disentangle him from his mood. 'Aren't we clever? Can't we work things out?'

'Yeah. Yeah. We can.' He took hold of her hands with their fingers that turned like strange twigs. 'We will work things out.'

'Let's enjoy it, Mark,' she laughed and looked him in the eye. Now was the time to tell him. 'I want to… make it even more difficult. I want you. I mean, you know what I'm saying, don't you?'

Embarrassment made her stutter.

'I want you too, Lin,' he said softly, still holding her hands. 'I do, I mean it.'

'But I want you. To be the first,' she said quickly. 'I'm a virgin, Mark. And I hate that. I'm not a totally soppy little innocent kid. I know things, I've read things.'

'I know. I didn't think you were… innocent,' he hushed then looked in silence at the rich brown leaves on the woody floor.

She waited a few seconds, exposed by her request. 'Well?'

'Oh Lin, what can I say?' His hands reached out and lifted her from the chair. Once on his lap, he carefully positioned her legs in a comfortable place. Soon they were kissing again, driving into each other. She was startled, and happy, to feel his cock tensing beneath her buttocks.

Holding around her back with one hand, he eased his other under her skirt and circled his index finger into her knickers. She was damp already.

'I want you to come for me, Lin. Now,' he murmured into her face and kept up the gentle movement. 'Trust me.'

'I do. Totally,' she whispered as she moved against his finger.

The sun played around them, creeping through the leaves.

His finger felt so different to the vibrator. The hot flesh was steady and unrelenting, pulling juice out of her. A deep tremble ran through her veins. Part of her was greedy for him to hurry, part of her wanted to hold back.

When the orgasm hit, Mark held her tight, pushing two fingers inside. She felt only slight pain – and a deep satisfying clench.

'Hungry beastie,' he laughed, pulling the fingers away and putting them into his mouth with a relishing expression.

She giggled, shocked and aroused.

'I think we have to arrange something for ourselves that is much more private,' he said, and helped her to sit up straight and began to rock his pelvis upwards against her bottom. 'There's something that wants to get much closer to you than this.'

'I don't know how we'll do it,' Linda blurted. 'You know, I have to tell you… my hips are really stiff. I just can't imagine how it's possible.'

'I refuse to believe it isn't,' he said, still moving gently. 'There's more than one way to try.'

'But we can't try out here, Mark,' she sighed, pressing herself down against him as hard as she could manage, excited to think of him, his cock, wanting her.

'We could sort something out, I know we could. But we'd need someone to help, someone from your unit, to give you a bit of cover. Is that totally ridiculous?'

'There's Jackie. She's a friend, too. I think I could trust her, really. She gets me out of trouble with all sorts of things,' she said at once. She couldn't give up on him now.

'Oh yeah, Jacks. I know her.' His voice was light. 'She's cool. She'll be perfect.'

His thrusts became forceful and he gripped her down hard on his lap.

'Doesn't it hurt?' Linda whispered, reaching her strongest hand to his face and enjoying seeing that his eyes were half-shut tiny points of light. 'I mean, rubbing like that. Can't you unzip yourself?'

'I'm scared we'll be seen,' he muttered but didn't stop the movement. 'We've been lucky so far. I don't want to be impatient.'

'No one will see while I'm on your lap,' she insisted, pressing his arm as she rocked her buttocks. He didn't reply but held her tight with an arm around her waist. Tipping her forwards slightly, in one urgent wrench he pulled down his zip with the other hand.

'With your legs together, Lin,' he half-laughed, half-mumbled. 'You can cover the evidence.'

She felt his cock now, a firm rod of flesh rubbing along the backs of her thighs. 'Don't drop me,' she giggled.

'As if,' he murmured, clasping her against him.

Now with his other hand free, he dragged her knickers to one side and played her clitoris in time with his own desire.

'Mark, Mark,' she snatched at his hand, finding a way that her fingers might grasp and keep him there.

His upwards rocking reached a steady but vehement rhythm. His breath almost stopped and he uttered several short grunts before rushing his hand away from caressing her, to propel his arm across her thighs, squeezing her down on his cock.

Linda felt him judder. Then, the warm stickiness was there along the back of her legs.

She felt alive and free, as the constraints imposed by the regime of the rehab centre fell away.

He smoothed his hand along the backs of her legs, edging a finger up from behind, slick with semen. She came quickly, clutching him with all the strength she could.

When she caught her breath, they sat laughing together, resting in the peace of the sinking sun.

'I bet you've made a right mess of my skirt, naughty,' she smiled, laying her head against his shoulder. 'I can't clean it up, you know. Haven't reached my own bottom since I was a kid.'

She let the words fall easily. What could it matter now? Mark's semen smeared across her skin, they had shared this moment. It wasn't so hard to fight embarrassment, it was irrelevant.

'Never mind. I've wiped up worse things in my time. I'll give it a dab if you want, to hide our dirty secret.' His hug was gentle, his voice a whisper.

'No, I want to keep it there. I want to smell it in my bed all night.' She lifted her head to smile again. It felt as if smiling was all she could do.

'We do have to go, though. Really. We'll be rushing. I'll take you back. Say I bumped into you in the corridor.'

'That's a new way of putting it.' She said, laughing, but felt cold at the thought of leaving him.

He lifted her back into her wheelchair in his delicate way. Before they came out into the car park they stopped behind a large oak tree and he kissed her again.

'Linda Jones, I want you,' he said, tightly, licking the tip of her ear as he swayed above her. 'I'm going to have you, and you sure as fuck will have me.'

As they moved from the wood onto the dry grey of tarmac, Linda noticed a swash of leaves fall down in front of them. She shivered and felt afraid of returning, struck with some instinct about the future. Sensing it was obvious the weather couldn't last.

*With the numbers on the female unit at a new low, only one night nurse was put on duty. She was a thin Chinese woman called Nurse Hoo, and left Linda to her own devices. There were none of the usual naggings to make her go through the undressing routine with the dressing sticks and implements supposedly to help Linda around the limitations of her movement. All part of the drill, part of boring rehab.

But tonight she didn't want to get undressed and revelled in the fact that Nurse Hoo didn't care. Laying under just a sheet, she breathed in the rich distinctive smell of semen and that of her own sexual aroma, now stronger and ever-present. She dozed in a dream of drowsy arousal, wondering about the details Mark had revealed of his past. And most of all, puzzling how Mark would solve the problem of *where.*

Next morning, as she was eased out of bed and wheeled to the table for breakfast by Nurse Hoo, relief buoyed her awake as she saw the sun was still out. Now she had to wait for Jackie's shift to start.

Hope dazzled her plans about the day ahead and the day after, but no longer than that because the real future had to be kept as far away as she could keep it.

When Jackie appeared she looked at Linda with wary eyes. 'Something's up,' she said quickly. 'You're in the shit over something. Prepare for the royal summons to Humpy-Face.'

Linda's stomach rolled and scenarios reeled through her head. Were they found out already? Would Mark be sacked?

The inner sanctum of the staff office was never exciting. Linda scanned the curling postcards, the endless post-it notes, stacks of reports on patients and two dirty white phones.

'This is a difficult one,' Staff Nurse Hampton began, looking out of the window.

Linda tried to stop her heart thumping so much in her throat and ears.

'There have been reports made to me that... you are not washing properly, Linda Jones. It is said that you smell rather badly at present.' The woman tilted her bulk to one leg, not looking at Linda.

There was a pause, the nurse sniffed close to her, and pulled a face of confused shock. 'Indeed, you do not smell very savoury this morning, young lady.'

Linda wanted to explode. The staff were always obsessed that everyone smelt, when the reality was that their BO was akin to chemical warfare. She wanted to look into the nurse's face and say, yes, she stank of semen, of sex and sweat, and that she wanted to stink of it some more.

Instead she took the sermon with a serene smile, as she thought of Mark touching her, pushing his cock against her body, his semen on her hands.

Later she willingly accepted help from Jackie to have a shower.

'I do smell, Jackie, I know I do. And I love it,' she said, as the young woman helped her slide over onto the shower-seat. 'I won't believe you either, if you say you can't recognise the smell.'

'God, you are so rude. But spill the beans, who is it? I'm bursting to know,' Jackie said, checking with nervous eyes that the door was locked behind them.

'Mark,' Linda whispered, abashed to tell someone else at last. 'We're meeting up in the woods. We're getting very friendly.'

'Mark is such a sweetie.' Jackie relaxed, turning on the shower. 'He's a gentleman, although not everyone likes him. He's too blunt and honest for his own good sometimes. But he's not a grunt. He won't piss you about, Lin, whatever else.'

'It has been a bit scary,' Linda said as she enjoyed the warm water soothing her body but hating that it was washing away the imprint of Mark. 'Jackie, I am so scared to ask, I know you could get in trouble. But would you help us? We want to, you know. He'll be my first.'

Jackie drew in a breath, preparing shower gel, but did not answer immediately.

'Please don't be upset, really, you don't have to help if you'd rather not. I'm sorry. It's just that I have to find a way of getting out of the unit,' Linda said, subdued with guilt. 'You know I'm not stupid. And you know how we always get treated here. They're so fucking obsessed with making our bodies normal, they can't see there might be other things we need too. Things other people just do without having to go through all this kind of palaver.'

'Look, don't worry about getting me in the shit. I can look after myself. But tell me what you think I can do? I want to help, I do. Tell me what's happening.'

'Mark's going to find somewhere we can go, I'm not sure where yet. But we can't just keep going off to the woods for an hour. Maybe I could say you've taken me out somewhere? Remember Sister Brooker let us go to the pub? They would let you take me out for the evening. That way I'd have cover and I could be with Mark and not worry.' She looked at Jackie with eyes wide and hopeful.

'Okay then.' Jackie grinned. 'I'm up for that. Why not? You should have some fun too, bossed around by the dried up old bags in here, week in and out.'

'I promise it'll all go smoothly. We'll make sure it does. If this lot weren't so uptight, it wouldn't be so difficult, would it? I am over age and I'm not making some sudden decision, Jackie. You've just told me Mark's okay. So what are you doing but helping me get around stupid rules?'

'Yes, it's all right, silly. Don't keep justifying it. I'm on your side.' Jackie wrapped a towel around Linda and turned the shower off. 'It's meant to be such an important thing, this first time business.'

'Oh, are you going to tell all, Jackie?' Linda bubbled over, dizzy, full of the sunshine knocking on the frosted window.

'No, some things should stay secret.' Jackie was serious. 'But you are a bit vulnerable. No, don't pull that face. Most women are anyway. You have other things going on too.'

'But I'm not stupid. You don't think I'm immature, do you?'

'I don't mean because you're disabled, not exactly,' Jackie said, and edged away from what she had started. 'Look, he's a nice guy. But even nice guys can hurt you. Neither you or him will be here forever. Don't jump in too deeply.'

Linda scrunched up her face. Anxiety could not be allowed.

'I'm absolutely crazy about him. But trust me on that one, Jackie. I want to do it. I don't care about the future right now. Not the far away future.'

'I'm happy to help, I mean it. You sort out with Mark what evening you want to get together. I'll sort out some kind of excuse.'

'Oh Jackie, you're the best,' Linda cried and wished her arms could move enough to hug her friend. Instead she leant forwards and surprised Jackie with a peck on the arm.

*

During the hard labour of OT therapy, Linda was drugged with the anticipation of seeing Mark. Her stomach grumbled and her hungry clit cried out between her legs. The sun was out intermittently, it didn't feel as warm and she saw that their times together in the woods would be cut short by the weather changing. There was no news on when she could go home. All other concerns were ignored by the spell in her blood and the drive in her head. To be with Mark, to have Mark.

She attempted to write a letter to a friend, but Miss Granston hovered too close as she tried to detail her relationship in rude, honest words. The barriers of the staff and their attitudes were always there, with the risks of crossing them. Risks of hurting Mark, it seemed, more than her.

When at last he appeared to take her back to the Unit, her heart raced. He helped her into the wheelchair and swiftly into the corridor.

'Mark, don't wheel me back. Let's just have a few moments in the disabled toilet in the outpatients. Please, baby.'

He squeezed her shoulder.

'Sounds promising to me,' he said.

The toilet was wide with the usual collection of bars at different angles. They didn't notice if it smelt, but fell on each other, yet Mark, as always, was careful, aware, moving to avoid hurting her. Linda loved how he made her feel but couldn't help cursing her body for being small and weak when she wanted to leap up and straddle him on the toilet, crushing away her virginity.

She made him stand up and release his cock for her to examine and touch, amazed at it, now presented with the smell, the hair and peculiar, crude fleshiness of a penis in front of her.

But then, she knew she was in love, or in love with love and the newly discovered allure of sex. Really, she knew her body would do fine, one way or another. Her initial distaste at his cock faded quickly and it seemed the most obvious thing to ease her strong tongue around the head and wriggle into the smooth foreskin. He groaned and supported her head but she knew she wasn't ready to do more. Instead she asked him to masturbate onto her breasts while she watched, breathless but distant, absorbing the sight with fascination as the semen pulsed out. She dabbed a cautious finger into it and then into her mouth, startled and amused at the taste.

They kissed again, the tang of his semen exchanged on it.

'I'll say I needed to go to the loo,' Linda said.

'What do you do to me, rude girl,' he sighed, stroking her hair as he spun the wheelchair back into the corridor. 'Let's hope Jackie can do her stuff soon. I'm working on the practical details. You make me so horny all the fucking time, I feel off my trolley.'

'I know,' she sighed. 'I know.'

Part Three

Six tortuous days passed of sneaking into the toilet, and once into the woods on a sunny day that fought back the gathering clouds. Six impossible days of mouths devouring, hands exploring, sweaty promises made, and conversations that danced between each caress.

The time was set for Saturday evening, Jackie fixing it to give the cover of a night at the cinema, which meant they would have five hours.

Jackie would help Linda get ready, take her out of the Unit, then Mark would meet her by their toilet.

When Saturday came, the rain came too.

'At least it won't matter,' Jackie said as she helped Linda to dress.

It was a ritual to attend to with loving care. Whatever happened, Linda felt, even if she returned from the night disappointed, her old life would fall away.

They were quiet as she prepared. The shower first, a drench of perfume. Her best bra, new knickers. Lacy stockings that didn't need a suspender belt, tracked down by Jackie.

'Will he like all this, do you think?' Linda asked. 'Is it a bit old fashioned?'

Jackie shook her head, smiling.

'Men usually like the undressing bit, you'll have no worries with that. It doesn't really matter anyhow. If *you* like it, then do it.'

'I am a bit scared, now it's coming to the crunch,' Linda said. 'What if I can't find a way, with my hips and stuff? I really dread that.'

'I've got a little present for you that should help with that problem,' Jackie said, pausing as she finished doing up Linda's black silk blouse. 'I was going to give it to you last thing, but you can have it now.' She bent down and retrieved a large book from a bag at her feet, putting it on the bed beside Linda.

The Joy of Sex by Alex Comfort.

'There's a bit on sex for disabled people, and beside that, a lot of pictures of people doing it in different positions,' Jackie explained, flicking the pages. 'I can't believe there's not one position you can find to do it in.'

Tears pricked Linda's eyes. She blinked them back.

'Thanks, Jackie. Thank you. This is brilliant. I don't know what to say. But we can have fun anyway, can't we? I want you to tell me though, does it… does it hurt, when they put it in?'

Jackie laughed lightly. 'Don't worry about it. You and Mark are so hot for each other now, that helps, honestly. But Lin, are you… safe? That's been bothering me, while we've been sorting this evening out. Mark could take care of it, but it might make it trickier. Another thing to worry about.'

'You mean contraception?' Linda looked up and smiled at them both in the mirror. 'What's funny about that is I'm on the pill, Jackie. Haven't I told you? I was bunged on it a few years ago, to control periods, I suppose. Bet the doctors wouldn't imagine I'd get something else out of it.'

'It's safe, though, you're sure?'

'Yes, Jackie. I've read the leaflet in the packet and all that. Promise.' Linda rolled her lips together and looked at her watch. 'Shit, nearly time.'

'You look great.' Jackie pulled a few strands of Linda's hair into place. 'I think you're going to have a wonderful evening.'

Linda stacked up a small handbag and Jackie put *The Joy of Sex* back in the carrier to hang on the handle of Linda's wheelchair.

'Have you and Mark spoken about me? Tonight, I mean?' Linda asked suddenly, not sure how she felt about that idea.

'Only briefly, to sort things out. He does care about you, Lin. He's not having a laugh or anything. He just isn't like that. He does what he wants and doesn't care about gossip and stuff, whatever he's up to,' Jackie said, her grey eyes steady on Linda.

'I care about him too. Maybe I love him,' Linda whispered, half-afraid to say it.

'Come on then, time for action.' Jackie said, laughing again. 'Let's go and get lover boy and find out about this mysterious location.'

*

Mark was dressed in black, the same as her. A t-shirt and tight black jeans, his face calm but his hands dancing.

'Thanks Jacks, you're the best,' he said absently, kissing her cheek. 'And Lin, Babe, you look absolutely luscious.'

'I'm sure there's a name for what I'm doing tonight,' Jackie said, chuckling and pursing her lips. 'And it's not a nice one.'

'Don't make me feel guilty, now,' Linda teased, because, of course, she wanted to be alone with Mark, and quickly.

'See you in five hours then. I'll be here,' Jackie said. 'I know you want to get shot of me.'

The area by the Outpatients Department was quiet and empty, shut down for the weekend. Mark gripped each arm of Linda's wheelchair and leant down to find her mouth. They kissed, a long agitated exchange of tongues and whispers.

'Lin, I wish this could be somewhere better,' he sighed as they set off along a corridor she had never been down.

'I know you warned me it would have to be at the centre somewhere, but where on earth have you found?' She was shivering, yet hot, not caring too much where she was going. Five hours anywhere with him would be enough.

'There's an annexe in one corner that isn't used now. Most of it is shut off, although it still has furniture and stuff.'

'Beds, I hope?' Linda's voice was dreamy. She knew she was gliding over some mysterious gateway and into another world.

'Wait and see, naughty.' He pushed her chair along but let one hand ease down to stroke her breast.

As they moved further away from the part of the centre she knew so well, she glanced outside and noticed darkness was falling.

*

The room was square with plain white walls. Two beds were pushed together in one corner and a long fat exercise couch stood along the other side. Battered boxes were stacked near the door. Everywhere on an available shelf, supplying low shadowy light, there were small candles and a faint dusty joss stick fought back the smell of dry old air. A cassette machine playing their favourite indie tracks pulsed in the background. Linda gasped, amazed at how much he had remembered their conversations, to know she would love this. On the two beds were piles of arranged pillows, covered with a deep red blanket. To one side, was a table with two glasses and a few bottles of white wine. A small electric heater whirred nearby taking the chill off the evening air.

Linda gaped. She had jumped into another dimension.

'Mark, you've made it perfect. This is so magical.'

'Let's get on the bed, Lin,' Mark crouched beside her and started undoing her blouse.

'I'm feeling a bit shy,' she whispered and lowered her eyes. 'We've never seen each other undressed. You'll see all my awful bits now, my peculiar body.'

'Silly, your bits won't bother me. You'll see mine too. It doesn't matter. I want you, Lin. Every bit of you.' He pushed her blouse down over her shoulders.

She noticed he was trembling. 'Lift me onto the bed then, undress me there.'

His strong arms slid under her legs and she flew into the air.

'Get comfortable. This isn't something to just get over and done with. I want you to enjoy it.'

'I will, Baby, I will.' She sighed and lay back on the bed with its nest of cushions.

He helped her move until she was settled. Then, kneeling beside her, he lifted his arms high to pull off his t-shirt. She made him move closer to touch the spread of hair in the centre of his chest, to feel it curl between her fingers.

Suddenly he swung over her. Keeping his weight on his arms, he lowered himself onto her lips. She lifted her slow hands to grab his hair, to ram her tongue into his mouth, and wished beyond wishing her legs would open to encompass him without complication.

He moved from her lips to drag his mouth into her loosened bra, finding her nipples, before leaning back on his haunches to rip open his jeans and let his stiff cock free.

'Do you think you could manage me lying on top of you? If I take most of my weight?' he asked, eyes shimmering in the shadowy light.

'I want to Mark, I want to try anyhow.' To deny ever feeling his body, warm and needy on hers, was unimaginable.

He jerked her black skirt up to her waist and pulled her knickers off in one movement. She felt exposed, a sacrifice for him, but was flushed and aroused. He lowered himself over her, his legs apart each side of hers, his cock stirring upwards on her bare stomach. The pressure put a flash of pain into her back but she shoved it away, gasping instead at the delicious torment of him being so close to her clit and waiting vagina.

'Okay Babe?' His breath was disjointed as he began to rock himself. 'You must tell me if I'm hurting you.'

'Yeah. It's all right, Mark, don't move away, not yet.' She moved herself against him to a level she could manage, as desire made her stronger than she could believe.

He rocked against her for a little longer. She hated the nagging pain in her back but remained silent. Unexpectedly, he jolted, and she felt a rush of wetness on her belly.

'Oh shit.' Mark moved back. 'Ooops. Sorry Lin. I'll clear it up. Got a bit too excited there.'

She lifted her head to peer at the stickiness and burst out laughing. He joined in as he dabbed tissues over the mess.

'You look so fucking horny lying there like that.' He stroked her stockinged legs, and she felt he was drinking her up. 'Don't worry, there's more.'

'Hope so. We've only been here 20 minutes.'

They laughed together. He lit up a joint and helped her smoke it before pouring the wine. Pausing, he removed more of her clothes. Kissing, exploring as new warmth enveloped her, aided by the wine and cannabis. Soon he was naked too and they lay down together, breathing each other in.

'I'm going to lick you soon, Lin,' he said lightly as he nuzzled her face. 'I mean, between your legs.'

She consented, tense with excitement but afraid that her body would not cooperate.

'Relax, Baby. Close your eyes.' He began to kiss along the top of her thighs, leaning across her at an angle.

She felt his breath on her pubic hair. His tongue plunged down as his hands held her thighs, which went into a vague disapproving cramp. Yet the sensation of his tongue shocked pleasure into the heart of her being. She began to moan as he circled into the tiny parted space her legs would allow.

Suddenly he stopped, made a rapid movement back to her mouth. She kissed him again and again, submerging in him and the strange tart taste from her own sex.

'Do you want to try and suck my cock?' he said.

'I'll try.' Some part of her was uncertain, but the feeling to know and discover was greater.

He knelt carefully over her chest, keeping his weight off her, then piled pillows under her head to raise her high enough.

She grinned at his erect cock so close now, long and smooth, the foreskin ending in a twist at the tip. He put his hand around it and began to rub. Linda urged forward and opened her mouth. Her jaw pulsed a complaint almost at once, as his cock edged in the space available. She concentrated to avoid biting him. His hands cupped around the back of her head as she used the strength of her tongue. It felt odd, yet stirred her, hearing his groans and sensing how much he wanted to push into her mouth. But she pulled back abruptly and her jaw clamped shut with a reproachful click.

'Sorry, I might bite you if I carry on. Try again soon?'

'There's plenty of time. I want to do something else. Trust me?'

She broke into trillions of palpitating pieces. 'You know I do. I'm here, aren't I?'

He kissed her stomach then helped her to roll on her side, putting pillows behind her back so she couldn't fall, getting her to pull her legs as far upwards as she could. She felt him lay down behind her, his feet reaching below the length of hers. He pressed all of himself against her, his pelvis tucked around her bottom.

'I'm going to try now,' he murmured and she felt him move, first his hands coming to her trembling vagina from behind. She closed her eyes, languorous with hunger, wine and dope.

His cock was there too, pressing between the cleft where her legs rested together. He eased it back and she felt something begin to part her flesh. She moaned and twisted.

'Don't move, Babe, don't move.' His words were compact and she felt his lust tighten inside them. 'This is all about connecting one bit to another.'

She couldn't help laughing as he tried to push into her. Somehow his cock slipped and butted against her thigh instead. He began to laugh too and fell back to fling his hand over her waist and pull her against him. They lay together on their sides, curled into each other. His cock pushed urgently against her buttocks and they rocked, joking and teasing.

'I've got that book.' Linda suddenly remembered. 'Jackie got me a sex book.'

He helped her sit up and brought it over.

'I wish we'd had this sooner, before today I mean,' he mused, keeping one hand between her legs, as they flipped through the pages together, chuckling at the drawings. 'There are lots of ideas here. We'll be fine.'

Linda felt herself turn sombre. 'Look, Mark, I love this, I love being here like this. But if we can't do it, then, you know. Don't worry about me. Don't be frustrated.'

'Lin, don't be daft.' He threw the book down and put his arms around her. 'This is only because it's the first time. We don't know each other yet, like this, sexually. It'll happen. And it'll get better.'

She made a hopeful sound, noting that he had no doubt there would be another time.

They drank more wine and she gritted her teeth through the embarrassment of him helping her go to the loo that was nearby. He said it turned him on, hearing her pee. Shyness was daft, she realised again, especially considering what they were doing.

'This book has given me another idea,' he grinned, eyes radiant, cock tense and ready.

With gentle arms he carried her to the couch across the room from the beds. He grabbed the pillows and blanket and made a new lair around them. He kissed her, flying his hands across her flesh, pinching the bud of her clit. Then when she was speechless and entranced, he helped her to lie down across, not along, the wide exercise couch, the crown of her head touching the wall on the pillow he placed there, as he held her legs firmly.

Carefully he lifted her legs up to rest along his body, and over his chest, keeping her knees straight. She liked the way she was supported against him with her feet just on his shoulders, and more than that, she liked the way her buttocks were positioned near the top of his thighs.

At once she realised what he was going to do.

'Let's try, Mark, I want you, I do.' She stroked his hands as he reached forward to tease her nipples again.

'I won't hurt you,' he said. 'You must tell me though, if you want me to stop.'

She smiled and closed her eyes.

His fingers tickled around her clit and slowly moved down to ease inside her. She whimpered. Then unmistakably his cock was there, within the folds of her most private flesh, opening and stretching her.

'I won't push it in more, just yet,' he said, swaying side to side, one finger winding over her gorged berry.

She knew he wanted to burst into her and climb over her body, digging his fingers into her skin. She looked into his eyes, overwhelmed with her own pleasure.

'Try some more. You're not hurting me.'

With one hand steadying her legs, he continued his attention on her clit while rocking his pelvis gently forward.

She felt a slither of constricting pain but didn't want him to stop. Her insides rippled and he pushed, while caressing her.

She made an effort to push back towards his cock and suddenly she knew it was inside her. Mark's finger pressed over her clit and she felt the rush of orgasm running furious and sweet in her limbs. There was more pain but she hissed it away as she came, fighting down, full of him as he began to ease in and out.

'Are you sure, Babe? Can I come?' he stuttered, sweat fresh on his torso, sticky on her legs.

'Yes!' She cried, shaking with the orgasm that had scarcely passed, holding her mouth together as the sharp squeeze in her vagina dulled under the excitement.

He groaned, throwing his head back, and pushed several times. That she didn't feel the precise action of him coming inside her – as much as she had imagined – was a surprise. But the semen was there, it was warm and real, fast in trickling away.

There was not much blood, no deep cutting agony. She felt relieved. They rested for a while to recover. Her genitals felt sore and her body ached from the novel activity. She knew she had to have him one more time before the evening caught up with them. As he turned to her again, with kisses and licks and coaxing words, the pain was much less when he entered her, and she relished that in their position he could rub her into coming when he was firmly inside her.

How she wanted to sleep with him, hear his breath through the night, to know he was there keeping her safe. And to wake up and have him again.

But time would not wait for them and they had to rush to meet up with Jackie. Linda laughed as Mark struggled to dress her. He said he loved her and she told him she loved him too.

Jackie hovered in the shadows by the outpatients.

'Everything okay? You look pleased with yourselves. At least you're back here promptly. I felt silly mooching around here in the dark.'

'No one's about, Jacks,' Mark teased, not taking his eyes off Linda. 'I made sure. And we're fine. Give us a moment?'

Jackie nodded and moved out into the corridor.

'Only till Monday, Lin, Babe.' He touched his head to hers. 'This is bloody crazy. I can't quite believe we've done it like this and managed everything.'

'Me neither,' she said, as a betraying tear burnt on her cheek.

It was dark and windy outside; inside the rehab centre was vast and empty. She would be a wreck until she saw him again.

*

It became obvious that Mark was right. Soon they were easy with each other, with his personal quirks and her boundaries of movement and strength. They scraped what time they could and fucked in the toilet, in their secret room, and even in the wood with her sitting backwards on his lap. She felt fevered, insatiable to experience all possibilities. For some days their hunger fed on this new intimacy, making them dizzy and greedy. Even when she felt sore and exhausted, still he could rouse her and still she craved him.

But a day was set suddenly for her to go home.

She told Mark at the first opportunity, sitting on his lap in the woods. She had not quite processed how she felt about it, in view of their relationship. The day was chilly and the layers of clothing prevented much chance of sex.

He stared at up her and said nothing for several moments. His mouth was compressed, eyes stony.

'We can still keep going though, can't we?' His words came at last. 'Could I come and see you at home?'

Linda laughed bitterly, and thought of her thin, divorced mother who lived on the brink of broken nerves. Linda was still the little crippled girl whose mother liked to give soppy teddies and fluffy purses, in an effort to stop the passing of time, and to challenge the sexy, black clothes and punky studded wristbands Linda loved. There was no chance of Mark grinding her down into the soft bed of her childhood, no chance at all.

'Let's just take things slowly, Baby,' she said into his hair. 'We knew this would happen. We can stay in touch, of course. But things will be different, they have to be.'

'Lin, I can organise something. I can travel to see you, it won't be too hard. Please say yes. What's the matter with you today? You're normally so keen. Don't make up difficulties, it'll be great! You'll see.'

He held her tight and smiled. But for the first time, the very first, she felt a strange waft of chilly irritation towards him.

*

He talked of trying to come and live near her. She surprised herself by feeling apprehensive. When they met now, he was obsessed with keeping things as they were. Weren't boys supposed to be tougher than this? Taking what they could and moving on to the next girl? It was a shock to accept she might break *his* heart.

Linda wondered if she had half expected it, and wanted it to end, even though she did feel wretched at leaving, at not having the heat of his hands and eager tireless body. And his mind, full of affection and easy intelligence.

At their last meeting, in their secret room, the sex was still good, yet she knew he remained distracted.

'I don't understand why you just want to chuck things in. Why we can't meet up?' he said, his arms slamming the air. 'We could do so much more, go out and all that normal dating stuff. I'm not pissing around, Lin, I think we have something good here. I'm not fucking ashamed of you or anything!'

'We can't, Baby, we can't.' Linda tried to calm him. 'There's just too much to get around. You don't know what it's like for me at home.'

He dropped his head to stare at the floor.

'We've got to be brave about this.' Her words fluttered, helpless things that wouldn't hold back. 'I think you should look for someone else, Mark. I'll be so far away.'

'I don't want anyone else, actually. This is so stupid. I don't understand!' He came back to her side, knelt down and embraced her. Too hard, she thought, much too hard.

She knew she couldn't say she loved him anymore.

On the day she went home, he came to see her on the Unit, clutching a small box that contained a spiky silver bracelet.

'I knew a punk-indie kid like you wouldn't want gold,' he tried to laugh but she saw his face was white and fixed.

She thanked him and kissed him goodbye, a full kiss, still overflowing with need. Neither of them cared at all if the staff saw them.

He walked away, not looking back.

*

Mark wrote her long, amusing letters for a while. He told her about the woods changing with the seasons, gossip about the other porters, and the juicy snippets that soon circulated about them. Linda replied at first, enjoying the continuation of his interest, particularly when periods of loneliness crushed hard.

She went to college for a year and passed all her secretarial exams. The letters to Mark became harder to write and she started to forget what he looked like, but felt she couldn't ask for a photograph.

For some time he stopped writing altogether and she thought of him only on occasion. She joined a group of disabled people campaigning for access in her town and attracted many admirers. She got a part-time job in a local animal rescue centre. After some months there, she had an affair with a young disabled volunteer, who cleaned out the animals and was hoping to return to uni to complete his training as a vet. She fell in love and thought they might live together one day.

Jackie stayed in touch for some months, then for a few years there was silence. Ringing up unexpectedly, she asked Linda if she could visit. The visits became regular and Linda would always ask about Mark, but Jackie would evade her questions, sadness in her soft grey eyes.

Sometime later, on one of the visits, Jackie revealed that she had gone out with Mark, after Linda had left the rehab unit.

'He moped for you for ages, he really loved you. It wasn't bullshit. But… we got together on the tail end of that. I think I felt guilty, I'm not sure why. I didn't mean to leave it this long before telling you, but it just got harder,' Jackie confessed. 'He was involved in some mad project to do with penguin numbers, you know what he was like with all that animal stuff. We haven't been in touch for ages.'

'I hope he's okay. I don't hear anything at all from him now, either,' Linda sighed. 'He was special and extraordinary. He gave me so much that is still part of me now. I hope he'll always know that.'

Outside, the rain that had fallen all afternoon, stopped in time with her words and summer sunshine came crisp and full of memories over Linda's pensive face.

Seven Days

Thursday

Fidgeting at the table in the drab Leyton restaurant, Lucy stared through the window wondering why she had ended up booking the place.

Russell's fingers pressed under the edge of her white stockings and the tablecloth formed a prim white apron shielding his actions from an elderly couple twitching cheap burgundy napkins at the small table near the door. Next to them, a loud father yelled at three noisy children.

Lucy smiled, enjoying Russell's reliable lechery. The stockings were for him to play with after all but she had too much pride to tell him that it had taken her an hour to get them on, using the hideous *official* plastic gadget that enabled her to drag them over her feet.

She fought away a groan as Russell's fingers pressed higher.

'Russ, please. I'll come if you keep it up. I've missed you so much, I'm ripe for it. Save it for later.'

'Okay, but I've got more planned for later.' Russell slid his fingers away, circling hard one more time.

She breathed in sharply. 'You bastard. I'm sure you have. Don't wear me out. Fatigue and all that?'

'More likely the other way around. I've already had half a day's work at the boring conference in boring Wembley, to get through, remember?'

'Well, I do love it when you visit in your stuffy suit. It makes me want to rip your clothes off and fuck you the moment you step through the door.'

'Why d'you think I come rushing around the North Circular, after that crap drive up from Kent, all sweaty and keen?'

'I've had to struggle today too, you know. No accessible bus available this evening, some fuck up with the ramp. So much for spontaneous freedom. The taxi cost me fifteen bloody squids.'

'I'll pay it darling. You know, boredom aside, I bow down to Mammon and he rewards me.'

'Don't show off. You really are impossible.' A waiter approached with their bill. She moistened her lips. 'Russ, kiss me, a proper kiss.'

He moved his chair and repositioned her crutches. Lucy sensed the other customers looking at them surreptitiously. Russell crouched and thrust himself over her mouth, a wide, urgent hand around her head. She ached into him, rolling a fierce tongue around his. Five months was a long, long time without him.

The waiter coughed an insolent full stop to their embrace.

'Your receipt, Sir. Thank you.'

Arousal burnt her flesh. She wanted him and wished they were at the flat. But unexpectedly, she was not happy.

A young girl shouted, 'Mummy, what's wrong with that lady's legs?' Mummy answered with a loud hiss.

'Any more news then?' Russell asked, furiously scowling at the woman. 'Five months is a long gap for us. Sometimes, Luce, I do wish things could be different. Emails aren't ever enough and you are so frigging unreliable. I like you to tell me what you've been up to and you've hardly said a word throughout the meal.'

'That goes both ways, you know. And you're so bloody secretive.' She felt helplessly pulled to stare at the road for inspiration. Outside it was moist and dark, and the rain was heavy.

'Yeah well, but you like my style.'

'Bighead. I suppose I do.' She sipped nervously from the remnants of her mineral water. 'I've been a bit bored, yes I know. As usual.'

'Bored is your middle name. Bet you've been a very naughty girl too.'

She looked away. Cars juddered along Lea Bridge Road, angry beasts having tantrums with each other.

'My doctor says I have a dodgy liver. Keeps asking me if I drink a lot, and of course I say no, not really,' she said giggling, steering away from seriousness.

'When you should say yes really,' Russell laughed, light-blue eyes scanning her face.

'I know it's mostly the shit he's put me on. I've read up on the literature.'

'But you can't come off it?'

'No, I'd have other problems. Pain and stuff.' She hauled away from his stare and began to play with the one remaining item of heavy cutlery. 'But it's my body, isn't it? My risk. You don't need anything do you, medication, I mean? Lucky you.'

'Madam, the drugs I indulge in are purely recreational,' he said in a dry, low tone, then leant forward to caress her hand as she fiddled with the ornate fork. 'At the moment, anyhow.'

'Let's change the subject. Not like us to talk about this medical shit, is it? We'd be thrown out of the disability rights movement.'

Outside, the traffic jerked forwards as the rain increased and the baleful streetlights spilled down an orange spew.

'A comfortable silence, eh?' He yawned and stretched his arms above his head. 'Not everyone can bear them.'

'I like them. I like them with you, Russ, especially. I'm just thinking about later,' she lied, when really she had suddenly remembered, for no particular reason, last Christmas and the big scene there had been with her mother. A stupid row about her not being married, and when would she marry, and why, in her circumstances, was she so fussy?

The traffic moved suddenly. Lucy felt dizzy from staring at the blur of headlights.

'Thinking about later when I thrust my tongue into your wet hungry minge? When you cry for more?' Russell pulled his lips together and poked out the tip of his tongue.

'You'll be crying for more too, Mr Ego,' she chided.

'I always want more, Luce. You know that.' He changed position to catch her gaze again. 'Look at you, gorgeous as ever. Fabulous brown eyes, that great, soft brown hair, and you always smell delicious. But you are not your normal self. A bit too ponderous, by Lucy standards.'

'Fuck off. I'm not entertaining enough today?' She scowled as her attention returned aimlessly to the traffic.

'Don't get prickly. I don't mind. I like a thoughtful woman. I just meant that you don't seem to be your usual bouncy self.'

The cars began to quiver into a watery mist as her eyes began to feel hot. She stared venomously into the street.

'I'm okay. I hate the winter. It makes me feel all peculiar.'

'More peculiar than usual? Don't let it get to you, my darling.' Russell reached out for her hand. She looked down at it, twisted to its own design, held lightly across his broad male palm. She glanced at his wide square face, thin lips twisted with humour. Gently she withdrew her hand. He was familiar to her as a lover, yet now he was here again, she felt uncertain. And in less than 24 hours, he would be gone.

The arrival of excited customers conveniently distracted them. An elderly woman edged her way across the carpet, stabbing her walking stick down, as clucking family members flapped their hands.

'I hate carpets,' said Lucy as they watched the woman sidle forward on fragile feet.

'Some are great for fucking on,' Russell whispered and stretched under the table to find her knee.

Pleasure zipped her skin. She was glad they were leaving soon, waiting only for the hot drinks they had ordered some time ago.

'Depends, really. I'm not so excellent on top with my creaky bits and pieces. Then there's the big problem of me getting on the floor. A total non-starter, Russ, don't you think so?'

'No, I don't think so, actually. And I'll bet you the luscious damp knickers you're wearing, that I can have you on the floor. Any floor.'

Lucy laughed, hating her anxieties. Listlessly she stared at the hateful rain tapping and querulous on the restaurant's windows.

At last, the waiter brought the drinks. Russell lifted her cup and asked in his most cutting, educated tones, 'Would madame like her tea poured now?'

'Madam most certainly would.' Lucy studied the meticulous movements of his hands, quivering to know they would soon deliver careful caresses over her.

As the tea splashed into the cup, she drifted back to their first meeting. They had found each other on a disability web forum, sharing tastes in music and a general relaxed outlook on life. Meeting up within a month of writing, intimacy was swift after the first kiss in the stuffy tearoom in Epping where she spilt tea on her lap. He chuckled gently at her embarrassment, and his slow deliberate kiss changed the reason for the deep glow on her cheeks.

Lucy shook herself and stared at her drink. 'I've missed you, Russell, I know you hate it when I tell you, but I have. When you've gone off again, it's like I've lost a favourite jumper. I feel all cold and… unsettled.'

'Thanks. I'm comfortable. Not exciting. Now I know why you like my visits. I keep you warm.'

'Don't be silly. You know there's more to it than that.' She hesitated, not sure of what she really wanted to say.

He drank his coffee in slow, fastidious sips. She watched, consumed with a tremendous urge to have him.

'Well, I can only stay till tomorrow, Luce. I don't like dashing off so quickly. I mean it.' He paused awkwardly, shaking his head. 'But you know what it's like.'

'I know what *you're* like.' She lapped at the tea without enthusiasm. It didn't matter, that was how it was. She told herself every time that it was okay; that some Russell was better than no Russell.

Putting down her cup, she admitted that he couldn't have stayed longer this time, anyway. Somehow, her diary was already bursting apart with friends, and there was Tom, faithful Tom, still hanging in there for a Saturday date.

Looking at him as he finished his coffee, she reassured him with a smile. She wouldn't be lonely. And tomorrow night at least there was Billy to keep her company.

*

Inside Lucy's flat they wasted no time and flew onto each other. Russell grabbed her onto his lap, a fast hand under her skirt, prising into her white knickers.

'Lucy, it's been too long,' he groaned. 'You're ready for something, what a damp little beast you are.'

She pulsed into his mouth and pressed her weight against his stiff cock beneath her, knowing that she was safe and supported in his arms.

'You make me wait, you fucker, I should hate you,' she cried, pushing her hands under his shirt, wanting to feel his skin. 'But you know I can't. You know it.'

'Come on, bedtime. I'm not wasting you on a quickie, even if my cock wants it.'

Russell's impairments did not affect his strength, so he helped her onto the bed. Lucy lay on her back, supported by the pillows he nestled around her.

'Time to tease these clothes away, though.' He grinned and slid his hands under her blouse, finding her nipples tensed.

'Do that thing you do, I can never get enough of that.' She gasped and closed her eyes, relishing his weight on the bed moving around her.

He laughed and began to caress a surgery scar that snaked along her right knee into her groin. Part of it was numb, some of it was over-sensitised. Russell's skipping fingers knew how to make this unique zone sing like no one else that she had ever known.

'Seeing as you've been so good, I think I can manage that.' He began stroking, light and imperceptible circles that made her writhe.

His tongue soon joined in, a snake probing into the warm wet hairs of her pudenda, around each nipple, behind each ear and across her neck.

'I want more of you, now. Kneel over me,' she said and straightened herself up, lying with a pillow under her head. 'Don't get undressed yet. I want your cock.'

She enjoyed the frisson of him being fully clothed above her and began to tremble as he unzipped and hovered his penis by her lips. Russell was an expert at not hurting her and held her head while she suckled at the tip, pulling the stiffness into her mouth as much as she could.

'Lucy, keep that up and I'll come,' he gasped, closing his eyes and grimacing.

She released his cock and smiled, petting her fingers along it and around his balls. 'My jaw's tired anyhow.'

'Shame, you enjoy playing with him so much.' Russell laughed and moved away quickly to dive his tongue into her mouth.

'Russell, get your clothes off, let's fuck. Please, darling, please!'

Russell deftly prepared a pile of pillows. 'Ready to roll then, darling?' he muttered. 'Let's get you in position for a little action. And I am rather partial to the view, I must say.'

He helped her onto them so that her face turned to one side on the soft mattress and her rear perched high over the mountain of pillows. Russell kissed each buttock before his fingers slipped between her thighs from behind, gliding over her labia and then her clitoris.

'Russell, don't tease me anymore,' she cried, muffled by the mattress. 'You've made me wait so long.'

'Just getting the old safety jacket on,' he panted, opening a condom packet, jostling around the bed into a kneeling position behind her.

As he pushed firmly, Lucy clenched. Russell groaned softly as he eased in and out, hands holding her shoulders and waist in turn.

This time she came just before him, the teasing and touching too much. The judder curled up her toes and her eyes rolled in her head, as the rain rammed relentlessly against the windows.

*

Grey morning was a pallid offering to wake up for, but when Russell's hand crept between her legs, she rolled away from the insipid light and towards his erection.

'I'll have to leave soon.' He was sleepy, pressing kisses into the fan of her hair on the pillow.

'Let's do it spoons-tyle,' she murmured, pulling his arms forward around her waist as she snuggled her buttocks against his cock.

Mysteriously, she found she could not come this time, and after Russell had finished he had a quick shower, while she dozed until he came to say goodbye.

'You know I can't promise when to see you next. I just don't know what's happening one day to the other.'

'It's okay.' She smiled and held his hand.

They both knew it wasn't. Russell looked down, roughly cut blond strands draping his wide face.

'No, I will try. It's not as though me and Karen are together. Not really. I'll try and move things on.'

Karen was the wife; the soon-to-be-ex-wife, divorcing Russell for adultery (and *not* with her). Lucy didn't want to bring *the wife* into the tension of their goodbyes. 'Just get here when you can,' she said, casually, as a rising pang of melancholy slipped into the bed in his place.

He leant over to kiss her, smoothing her hair. 'No, I mean it. I'm going to sort something out. I'll ring later today to say hello. Promise.'

Promise. Lucy had learnt to not pay much attention to Russell's use of *that* particular word.

Friday

At work, Lucy relished the secret of her aching thighs and bruises. Looking up at John working at the desk opposite her, she wanted to scream how she was happy to be fucked sore and tired through each part of her being.

Her manager had grey hair, cut like a bad toupée and a large, wide suit that made him look like a strange teddy bear striped in greys. She speculated that John had taken in his disability equality training and that he kept a notebook of politically correct language in his desk drawer. Did it have *disabled people fuck* in it, she wondered, tapping idly at her computer? Could the boring old suit-man process *that* idea?

'Okay Lucy?' He beamed at her unexpectedly.

'I'm fine, John. Very well indeed. In fact, you'd never guess–'

She stopped, and a heavy silence ran through the office as strings of brown hair fell over her face and her mouth shrivelled shut.

'Never guess what, Lucy? You haven't been boozing again, have you?' He looked at her with a bright rosy face.

'Yeah. Yeah, I know I shouldn't,' she mumbled, eyes rigid, locked to the screen.

'You *are* a bad girl, aren't you? We can't complain about your work, though. You do the best reports in the office.'

She managed a terse smile and hung low over the keyboard. 'Better get back to work then, can't let those standards drop,' she said limply, her typing taking on a frantic beat.

A few minutes later, Terry brought over a coffee. It struck her now to wonder why she hadn't thought about him much before, when every week they slid their chat further along flirty pathways. She perked up, enjoying the way his thin mobile fingers tapped the desk.

Something stirred, but she stole it away to ponder later. Billy was due at her flat at 8.30 after catching a train from Hackney Wick. She couldn't get distracted.

'Lucy, come on, Babe, let's have a chat at lunch one of these days. Go on.' Terry winked at her and moved back slowly towards his desk using a pair of walking sticks. 'Us lot should stick together in these faceless council offices.'

'All right then, soon,' she grinned, running a pen around her lower lip. Terry was tasty, it was undeniable. But he was spoken for, after all. He had mentioned a girlfriend, she was sure of it.

'Maybe next week sometime. I'm just so busy.'

Rain made patterns on the window next to her and twilight curled fast fingers into the grey clouds. She remembered that she had forgotten to call her mother, startled to realise it had been over three months. Tomorrow she would make an effort – if she could squeeze the time out of the day.

*

Billy arrived with pockets bursting with adult candy and a rucksack full of booze.

Lucy sighed in disappointment. 'Red wine, Billy? You know that makes me puke.'

He widened his eyes and scratched his scattering of black hair. 'Oh sorry, forgot. What about this though?' He shook a little packet of white powder.

'Billy, you know I don't do coke either. My sinuses hate it. I'm too snotty. I'll guzzle the shitty red poison. You can sniff your septum away.'

'I had an incident on the way here, so I was a bit distracted,' he said as he skilfully prepared a line. 'I stopped at a pub, near the station. As I went in this fuck-brain shouted, "Serving shorts today, are we, ha-ha", with all his buddies sniggering into their beer. I thought, should I, you know, say something?'

'And did you?' Lucy screwed her face up as the coke vanished into his nostrils.

'Nah, I couldn't be arsed. Not this time. Didn't want to be late, either. So I let him off.'

Lucy sat in the lounge on her favourite chair that was high enough for her to use without difficulty. She realised her knees were throbbing but ignored them and threw the wine into her stomach. As it tumbled down, like bad water into a sewer, she remembered her medication and realised it was two hours late.

Night drew down a rapid curtain as they sat peacefully in the darkness, a single candle on a small table between them.

There had been an 'incident' on the day she had first met Billy, and it threw them together into a light, casual relationship. At the Royal Festival Hall, almost a year ago, a middle-aged woman with high, frosty hair and a dull, plummy voice had barged up to Lucy, as she waited for a show to start, insisting that she recognised her from the local *handicapped* club in Richmond where she did voluntary work. At a nearby table, Billy sat shaking his head sympathetically.

The woman had ended by declaring, 'Well, your sort must all have the same look about you.' With that, Lucy sidled off to the sanctuary offered by Billy and his table. They soon became fuck-mates and were happy with the arrangement.

Billy rolled another joint with fast fingers, which he lit and passed to her carefully.

'You like this though, don't you, Lucy my darlin'? Good skunk it is.'

'Hmmm.' She drew on it, an effervescing heat warming through her being. 'Let's have another snog then, for fuck's sake.'

He stood between her thighs and she leant towards him from the chair, fighting with his keen lips.

They ordered an Indian takeaway. Lucy took her pills with a gulp of the sharp red. More joints were shared. A fast blow job for Billy and a rushed tonguing on a bruised clit supplied the diversion she had hoped for but reminded her too much of already missing Russell.

Time split away from them as darkness started to crush against the windows, shocking her with thoughts of winter. She had a feeling of having missed something; of a thought lost to the void, and realised that Russell had not rung. Billy lay across the sofa, blinking. Her tabby cat, Stripy, sat between them, curled into his own oblivion in the middle of the green carpet.

'You were going to play me something. Some blues thing you had. Memphis Minnie.'

'Was I?' Thoughts wrestled with the poor visibility in her brain. She could not remember. Did she have that record?

'Everyone wants to buy my kitty.'

'What? What are you on about?' She began to laugh. The words vanished quickly into the fog.

'The name of the song, silly. You said,' Billy muttered, closing his eyes.

Silence lay over them like a comfort blanket.

'Lucy.' Billy pushed the comforter away. The sound of her name screamed out. Stripy stood up suddenly and stared through the window at the thick darkness outside and endless invisible cat things.

'Yes?' she replied with effort.

'Do you… do you think you're happy? Or, well, just okay about things. In your life. You know.'

The wind pounded against the door and the cat leapt into the hallway. Lucy staggered to her feet, grabbed her crutches and dragged herself to the bathroom. The red wine splattered into the sink, sour and curdled with curry and undissolved pills.

Saturday

Lucy woke up to the intercom drilling noise through her ears. She wasn't sure where her arms were and located them by the strange stiff pain in her fingers. Slow and shaky, she pressed the button on the bedside phone, stunned, briefly, that she didn't remember getting into bed.

'Come in Helga. I'm… not great.'

As her morning assistant bounced into the kitchen with a cheery, 'Good morning', Lucy wondered where Billy had gone. It did not matter – all her workers were used to finding guests everywhere – but she would have preferred a proper goodbye.

The wreckage of her body would not resurface with any speed. As she flopped into her wheelchair with Helga's assistance, she noticed the scrap of paper on her bedside table. It said, *Luce, we both got a bit too wasted. Hope you bounce back pronto. Will text. Don't get too off your face tonight. BE HAPPY. cu soon. Billy x x.*

She squirmed at the two capitalised words. Nausea sprung from the jittery trampoline of her guts. Pushing away the note, she mumbled an instruction to Helga for coffee. Thankfully, it was Saturday. There was a lot to do before she recovered enough for Tom that evening.

A growing list of calls stared accusingly from the notepad as she tentatively munched a dry slice of toast, but she knew they would have to wait a little longer. Swallowing down her disappointment with breakfast, she told herself Russell would not ring.

*

Tom's large, sleek saloon car was full of snug upholstery and seats that went to full recline. It was 3am, and damp London glowed below them in the pinpoint bloom of street lighting and the lonely movement of headlights on straying solitary vehicles.

They parked on the road at the top of Alexandra Palace and together stared at the scene sprawled out before them while nibbling on a box of chocolates he had bought her.

'I never get tired of it,' Lucy said.

'What? London or chocolate?' Tom stretched down to tease along her thigh, circumventing the limitation of his short arms' reach.

'Neither, actually. Look at it. All spread out. At least the rain's almost stopped, although I can't see The Eye. Look, Tom. Do you want a blow job or something soon? Or are we going back to my flat for a fuck?'

There was one beat of silence. Tom made a strange sound. 'Lucy, don't. You make it sound so… so unromantic. I want to fuck you into the bed, of course. But–'

'We could try in the car, though I've never managed that before. Hips too dodgy and things always dig in. And we'd have to move from here, of course. Maybe go to some part of Epping Forest. I know all the best places where we won't be seen.'

'Lucy, you are incorrigible.' Tom stroked under her skirt, his head leaning against her. 'You *know* what I want. I don't suppose it's worth asking again. You must think I'm a right old-fashioned geek!'

Lucy drank the last drops of her Archers and rushed in a breath. 'Tom, I don't know how to tell you this. I don't want to hurt you all the time.'

Another thump of silence. Then, Tom prompted, tentatively, 'Well, go on.'

'I fucked someone else on Friday. And I was with someone last night.'

The words formed a cloud, obscuring them from each other.

Immediately, she wondered why she had been so brutal. 'Look, this is silly. I go off the rails. You forgive me. Even though I know it kills you. Then we pick up things for a while, but I'm hardly faithful wife material, Tom. I just can't change how I am.' She almost said *for you*, but stopped the stab of her knife.

Tom took his hand away from her thigh, sat up straight and started the car engine. His fingers curled around the adapted steering wheel. 'What the hell do you expect me to say to that? I mean, I don't understand why you want to see me, really, if I'm just some notch on your bedpost. I suppose I always hope you might change. That, oh, eventually love might come into it.'

'You're not just a number, it's not like that,' she said, looking at the creases in her skirt, which she couldn't straighten from the angle she sat at. Her mouth scraped empty. There would never be love between them – not that desperate, needing, giving kind that meant a life together, commitment and maybe children. The type of life Tom wanted.

'What *is* it like then? I actually want to understand. It's not a crip thing, surely?' He flinched his eyes towards the crutches on the back seat and lifted his short arms in an angry gesture.

She sighed, exasperated. The situation was a variation on a theme. 'No, fucking hell! Of course not. I can't–' her voice wavered and she shook her head. 'I can't be pinned down. And I play safe, always, don't worry about that.'

Tom shrugged, making a sharp noise under his breath. Silence fumed through the car. Lucy watched as the headlights of a vehicle meandered along in the direction of Tottenham. Everything that came to her mind to make things better stuck like a foul sore on her tongue. She turned her attention back to the interior of Tom's car, fixing onto the old newspaper on the floor near her feet and several empty bottles of Bacardi

Breezer. The alcohol was already beating her stomach to a pulp but she still wished there was more.

Tom sat with his head down, the engine purring expectantly. 'You make me feel violent, Lucy. I want to push you down in that seat and–' She saw that he shook as he fought to manacle words together. 'I need to know whether we're together or not. I mean, a couple, stupid as it sounds. I see you every week, and I've always been aware you're not a bloody nun.'

'Tom, we go over this so often I get really tired. I *do* care about you. A lot. But I can't get married. It's a stupid idea. For me, anyhow.'

Tom didn't answer, but swung the car onto the road. Silence skulked alongside them until they were on the North Circular, rushing east.

'I'm sorry, Tom, I am,' she whispered and wished she could turn enough to touch him. 'I don't want to hurt you. All the time. I need you to see that I'm not right for you. And for marriage.'

'Shouldn't I decide that?' he replied, voice low.

'Let's go to the forest, anyway. We can play around a bit. Half the fun is in trying, you know that. We've never been about straight fucks, anyway, have we?' she coaxed, hating the place where she had plummeted them both.

Tom sighed. 'You are in such a strange mood. I want to say no. I do. I want to punch your pretty little head in. But you know I won't say no, don't you? I want what I can get of you.'

Lucy closed her eyes. The beat was in her ears; the familiar heat between her thighs. Tom, with his handsome pin-up face, his mobile mouth and taut, muscled thighs. She wanted some more of him, too.

Funny how it was Tom her mother wanted her to marry; that *he* was at the messy centre of that row, but thankfully did not know it.

Sunday

After Tom dropped her off in the morning, she managed to fall onto the bed fully clothed. Melting together, they had kissed and touched, orgasms licked and sucked into life, watched by the bare bristling trees at High Beech as the sky trembled to a feeble dawn. His smell wrapped around her and she burnt from his helpless love. With a tiny pang, she regretted it was not mutual.

Outside, a bird reminded her how late it was, and how much she lacked decent sleep. She knew it was likely she would lose Tom. He wanted something she couldn't give, and as she drifted into sleep, she decided, for perhaps the hundredth time, that she could not see him again.

Inside a light doze, she heard the phone ring and the voicemail click on. She tried to rouse herself, tensing with the anticipation of hearing Russell. Instead, her mother's nervous voice whispered, 'Hello, are you there? It's Mum, Lucy. Are you all right? It's been ages.'

*

The evening was calm and clear, with a big gold moon hanging low in the sky. Lucy wrote some emails, including a long lustful one to Russell, admonishing him for not ringing, hiding disappointment behind lewd jokes. The TV relaxed her for another hour, with Stripy on her lap.

As long shadows fell into her bedroom, she decided she had to get dressed. Martin, a friend from her evening pottery class, was expected. As she went through her wardrobe with Peggy, her evening assistant, she veered towards cancelling. Lucy had done her usual thing – saying yes without thinking; without considering. It was not a date; he was just coming for a drink. Yet she liked the confident way he used his white cane, and he *was* clever and always had plenty to say.

Putting on a black skirt and a velvet blouse, Lucy insisted to herself in front of the mirror that she did *not* fancy him; that the visit was not about *that.*

But when he flipped his hands around her body, she found her greedy senses responding. He eased up her skirt with perfunctory finesse and coaxed her quickly for penetration. They laughed their way through putting on the condom, with the difficulties their different impairments presented.

Sex was over in minutes, and she passed him tissues to clean himself up. He kissed her a few more times and told her she was wonderful. They shared too many drinks, and when she was about to ask if he would like to stay for a late takeaway, he said he had to get home, but that maybe they could get together again, soon.

Lucy wondered why. Why had it happened? But it was dangerous to analyse, and she put the thoughts away at once.

Monday

Monday morning brought another throbbing hangover, and Lucy stayed in bed until midday, having asked Helga to ring up work and tell them she was sick. She lay still for as long as possible before straining up to have assistance with a shower. By the afternoon, a stronger breeze returned to press against the windows, reminding her how much she hated this time of year, when Christmas threatened early with its obligations and fake jollity. She stayed in her nightclothes and read, feeling bored as she recovered slowly.

That evening she had Kevin down for a visit. An old mate from college, he was in her bed within the hour, breaking her open like an overripe fruit.

Getting rid of him as quickly as she could, she slept on the sofa to avoid smelling him in her bed. Stripy came and sat on her lap, vibrating his loud deep purr. 'Stripy, it's a real kick. But really, why? Why do I do it?' The cat gazed at her and blinked. Lucy laughed and tickled his head. After eating a packet of biscuits, she dozed in front of the TV, drowsily aware that Russell had still not called.

Tuesday

Back at work, she felt sick at the thought of food and tried her hardest to hate men, firing off emails when she could, to tell a number of them to go fuck themselves. The words on her screen blurred into incomprehensible patterns, and after a few hours of the dull distraction of inputting data, Terry jaunted up with a coffee. He had on grey, well-fitting trousers, a blue shirt, and – she couldn't help it – he looked very attractive indeed.

'You're a bit pale and weary today, Luce my sweetie. Skived off yesterday, too. What's up?'

'Rushed at the moment,' she said, wondering if she could have him too.

Terry put his slim walking canes against the table, perched on it and began to circle a finger.

'Have lunch with me, then?' He put his hand on her shoulder and squeezed. Lucy looked up. John wasn't at his desk. In the near distance, a printer whirred and outside the wide glass windows, the winter winds blew.

'Not really hungry today, if I'm honest. But I'll share a mineral water with you.'

'It's a date,' he said. 'I'll give you some light relief by telling you my boring problems.'

She laughed her best laugh and held his stare for a few seconds.

Over the mineral water, she remembered there had been a girlfriend, though it now appeared there wasn't. Lucy listened as Terry laid bare his worries over the *ex's* motives for leaving. Had he been dumped because he was a crip *and* black? Had Dee ever liked him for himself?

Lucy kept her eyes on his face. She touched his hand. In the empty canteen, as they went to go back to the office, they kissed. She breathed him in, dazzled by the way he cupped her face and held her still as they lingered in each other's mouths.

'Don't speak,' she hissed, seeing his pleased, quizzical expression. 'I don't like questions. Go with the flow, Terry. Go with the flow.'

'But Lucy, this… this is a bit–'

'I know, it's a surprise. I'm full of them. Let's be discreet. Meet me at the entrance at five, if you can.'

'Why?' He stroked her hair away from her face, deep eyes trying to look inside her head.

'You'll see. I might have another surprise for you.'

His laugh was rumbling and dry. 'Not sure I can take another one, Lucy, I'm a bit fucked up with Dee chucking me. I'm not sure—'

'Shhh,' she smiled and caressed his hand. 'Go with the flow. I'll see you later, then?'

'Well, yeah, of course. Why not?' he grinned and kissed her quickly.

She returned to her desk, seething with a desire that chased away boredom with the thought of hot hands, and smudged the hard lines of disappointment she felt that, still, Russell had not rung, or even emailed.

*

At five, Terry was there at the door, hunched, tapping his walking sticks, not catching her eyes. Lucy positioned herself against the wall, holding onto her rucksack with a struggle, angling her crutches to be able to support herself enough to tug his arm.

He didn't resist, but looked at her mournfully. 'Babe, I think you're wicked and sexy and all that, but we–'

'The feeling is mutual, honey. Without the but.'

'I'm not sure what I was playing at. I don't want to mess–'

'Stop it, silly. Come with me.' She waved a key at him. 'I've wangled us a quiet little place for some privacy. We can chat more there.'

He acquiesced with a half-hearted wave of his hand as she slipped her crutches back on and led him down a long corridor to a small alcove with a door at the back.

'This should suit us fine. I told Daddy John I needed to catch up with the work I missed yesterday. Preferably in a quiet place. He was most impressed.'

'You *are* cheeky, aren't you?' Terry came into the room behind her. She smiled, chest contracting, as he casually eased his hand over her backside.

The room was a small square with a table in the centre, foggy with dust. There were two padded typing chairs pushed against one wall, headrests hung low. One filing cabinet, a drawer half-open, stood derelict in a corner.

Lucy sat on the table, putting the crutches to one side and flinging down her bag. Terry wavered by a chair, not looking at her.

'Give me a kiss then.' A terrific flush flowed through her blood. She would not accept a refusal.

He moved closer, leaning his sticks to one side, touching her knees with his thighs. 'I don't know, you *are* a bad girl,' he sighed but bent down to find her mouth.

Lucy clutched him.

'Go and lock the door,' she hissed, pushing her hands to their limits to feel his body. 'And put a chair in front of it, too.'

He obeyed as if hypnotised, then returned to her face, his strong arm pulling her forcefully to his mouth, his weaker arm slipping into her top to find the softness of her breasts.

'We can do it, now,' Lucy breathed. 'Terry, I want to. Let's try.'

He eased one knee between hers. She leant towards him and felt his straining cock.

'Don't say no.' She rocked, dangling her legs around his thigh, rubbing herself against it.

'Oh, Lucy, isn't it risky?' he muttered, joining her rhythm. 'I don't know, should we?'

'There's hardly anyone here. I'm making up for lost time, remember?' She laughed. 'We won't be disturbed.'

'How then? Tell me.' His voice strained into her hair and he pushed his cock against her body.

'Help me get my knickers down, please. That's it–'

His hand swooped under her skirt, fingers exploring her warmth. Then he paused, suddenly. 'I haven't got a condom on me.'

'I have.' She squeezed him playfully and ordered him to sit on one of the typing chairs while she rummaged in the rucksack.

'Get close to the table. Unzip.' She watched him with feverish eyes, handing him the condom.

'This isn't as easy as it looks,' he grinned, biting open the packet and trying to unroll it with his most mobile hand.

'I'll help,' she said, bending down precariously to hold his thick, long penis. Her thighs trembled as he unravelled the condom.

'I'm going to try to ease back onto you now, leaning on the table.' She let go of him and turned herself around. 'It's all a matter of getting the angle right.'

She felt his cock striving keenly and tried to adjust herself towards it. Between her legs, she was wet and open, rabid for him.

'Luce–' Terry stuttered, thrusting towards her. 'I'll hold you as best I can.'

Suddenly she felt his cock was there and she let herself slide backwards. He filled up the greedy space inside her and she cried out. Terry began to rock upwards into her, breathing heavily across her neck.

The chair began to move backwards towards the wall, veering under their combined weight and motion.

'Shit! Careful,' Terry laughed, his arm gripping her waist.

'Fuck, I'd better move.' Lucy joined in his laughter. 'We can't have a scene where I need rescuing from the floor. Edge the chair back to the wall and I'll get up.'

Reluctantly she heaved away from his cock, and staggered to her feet. 'I'll lean forward over the table. That has been good for me before, Terry. You're not too much taller than I am. Get it in from behind. I'll lean my head on the rucksack.'

'Oh, Baby,' he said, sighing as he ran his hands over her buttocks. 'I'll just check the condom... okay... let's try.'

He sank into her with a groan. Lucy gritted her teeth as the edge of the table cut into her thighs. She ground herself against him with as much energy as she had. The rucksack was hard and uncomfortable, digging into her forehead. She ignored it and screwed her eyes shut, shunting back and forwards on the table. Abruptly his hand dived around, scrabbling for the burning centre between her legs. He jabbed at her clitoris and she grunted.

She felt Terry push harder, keeping a regular rhythm. He came with a sharp sudden cry and pushed his fingers over her clit. She burst into her orgasm.

'Fuck, fuck, ouch!' He ripped out, swearing and laughing. 'My leg's gone into cramp. Fucker!'

She laughed and turned over to face him as pleasure shook her body. 'Shhh, naughty. Trust you to get a cramp. Didn't ruin it I hope.'

'No way, babe.' He pulled away the condom and took the tissue she offered, idly screwing both up into his jacket pocket.

They sat recovering their breath, grinning at each other. Lucy stuffed her knickers into the rucksack. He had been good, and she was satisfied.

They crept out of the office, giggling and kissing.

'We'll get together soon, then? Properly?' Terry grinned, waiting with her for a taxi as the winter wind blew his words around her head with foreboding.

*

As the taxi drove Lucy home from the plain Walthamstow street, she marvelled gloomily that she found herself imprinted with another man's smell. She was hardly happy, and the tears she felt she should cry hung uncooperatively from dry, gritty eyes.

Her assistant made her a quick dinner, and after a few hours of TV, she picked up the list of calls to make. *Mum* sat accusingly at the top. To one side, she had scribbled, *Russell,* half over it. With as much strength as she could muster in her small hands, she pressed the pen down to scratch out both of them.

In bed, she stroked the cat with a tired shaking hand, murmuring between tight lips. 'Men are so cheap, Stripy, so fucking easy. Just like me.'

In the uncompromising darkness, the answer machine blinked an accusing red eye.

Wednesday

Wednesday arrived with the pitiless winter sun blasting through her bedroom window. As Lucy prepared for work, a drum thumped painful rhythms in her head. She knew she needed more sleep and solid alcohol-free rest. There was no chance of skiving off more work, especially when John would have expected that she caught up.

Terry would be there at work, hanging around her desk, a certainty she would have to deal with. He appeared within minutes of her arrival and perched on her desk, bouncing a walking cane on the floor.

'You're in your wheelchair today, are you okay?'

'I'm fine. Just rather tired, that's all.' She kept her eyes on the screen, speaking rapidly.

'Not surprised. I was knackered after yesterday's turn of events,' he laughed, a low pleased sound. 'You all right about things though, Luce? No regrets?'

The line she was typing came out full of errors. She kept her eyes on the keyboard, fingers hovering. Background voices boomed, a woman laughed, a door slammed shut.

'Can we talk later, Terry? I know John wants this finished before lunch.'

'What about coffee soon then? Johnny boy won't mind. Babe, he wants to adopt you, he loves you so much.'

She looked up at his keen expression and went cold. He winked and put his head on one side waiting for her to speak.

'Okay then, at eleven.' She gave in, knowing that they *did* have to talk; that the hunger of the moment had passed for her; that, perhaps cruelly, she did not want him any more.

*

The harsh sun driving brilliance through the window blinds set off a migraine, as she sat by the coffee machine sipping from a weak tea. Terry sat beside her with a coffee, his eyes never moving from her face.

'It's my fault. But I don't think we should have got carried away like we did,' she began, looking down into the plastic cup.

'It was a bit sudden,' he grinned, trying to catch her eyes. 'I'm happy to take things slowly, don't worry.'

Lucy put the cup on the table too firmly, spilling some tea as the bright sunshine swamped her tender head.

'I don't think we should really take things anywhere, Terry. I'm sorry.'

She moved her wheelchair to find some comfortable shadows.

Terry frowned. 'Babe, I don't quite understand. What about yesterday?'

She picked her cup up and dripped tea onto her skirt. 'Terry, yesterday was just one of those things. A fuck. Maybe a stupid, spur-of-the-moment thing.'

'Well, I didn't think it was stupid.' He turned his head away, furiously drinking his coffee. 'I'm not that cheap.'

'And I am?' she flared. 'We had sex because we wanted to, didn't we? Don't build it up into something it's not, Terry, please.'

He turned to look at her again. She flinched under his confusion.

'I thought, maybe, as we like each other, that, well –'

'That what? It would lead to more? More convenient sex at work, or what? Don't try that little number on me.'

Silently he slapped down his coffee cup, a puddle staining the table. He stood up slowly with a dismissive gesture and walked away.

'You're fucked in the head,' he said. 'A disappointment.'

'Fine. We know where we stand then,' she said loudly to his back, straining her tired arms to move her wheelchair back to the peace of her desk.

*

Lucy had almost forgotten Vic was visiting that night, for the pictures, maybe, and then a meal at home.

The sun set into a subdued early evening and she noticed that the radio was broadcasting Christmas announcements.

Slow and tentative dialling her mother's number, she thought about cancelling Vic, but hearing the engaged tone, she cut off the line and went to the bedroom to decide what to wear. Vic was usually good for long conversations, so she knew she could air a few grumbles about life, though she told herself she would *not* sleep with him.

'I won't, Stripy. I can say no, can't I?' Lucy smiled at the cat nestled into the bed. She let the assistant leave and with a few minutes spare before Vic was due, she tried her mother's number again and got the answer machine.

Susan, neglected Susan, was next on the list. Russell, he could go and fuck himself on his promises.

'Hello Luce, it's been ages. What on earth have you been up to, you ol' bag?'

'Oh, Suse, I've got someone over in a min, but can I book you in soon? There's so much to catch up on.'

'Yeah, sure, tomorrow if you want. Not too late, though. Who's the date, by the way? Not that Tom bloke, is it?'

Lucy cringed and dashed a look at her watch. 'No, Tom's not really in the picture anymore. But it's not really a date. Vic's coming over, do you know him?'

'Isn't he that trendy artist bloke? Blondish, brown hair. Likes a leather jacket and chain-smokes. I've seen him around at someone's party, I think. He's quite tasty, isn't he?'

A loud knock on the door stopped Lucy's answer. She rushed her goodbyes, checked her hair in the mirror and went to answer it.

*

As Vic came in, she realised at once he was a bit drunk. He kissed her fiercely in the hall, making her teeter on her crutches. She accepted that advance, surprised but intrigued, reeling in the smell of alcohol and cigarettes that hung on his clothes. They shared some drinks and she suggested they should get ready for the taxi she had pre-booked. He coaxed her to cancel it and said he felt like staying in and talking, which they did for half-an-hour until, as they sat close to each other on the sofa, he said he wanted another kiss.

She felt a distant arousal, blurred by curiosity and the veiled intentions in his weathered face. A murmur at the back of her mind resolved to resist anything more.

He pushed her down onto the sofa suddenly, his greater height and mobility no match for hers. She tried resistance as the initial hint of desire fled. She didn't want him and *wasn't* going to have him.

Yet he crowed words into her hair, ripped away her knickers and crushed his weight between her stiff, exhausted thighs. He lunged inside her, ripping her open, and when she cried out in pain, he grasped her face hard, nails sharp. Blood burnt on her cheek. She whimpered, taking herself somewhere in her head till it was over.

He came quickly with a hideous grunt, moving off her with a leering smile. 'I knew you were hot for it,' he chuckled as he zipped himself up. 'Shall we try and make the cinema now? There's probably a late screening.'

Lucy trembled. She could not look at his face.

'Please, just go.' Her voice felt weak, a million miles from her body. 'Just go.'

He moved towards her, face querying. 'What? Why? You were up for it. Don't kid me, Lucy. I know you. I've heard what you're partial to.'

'Get the fuck out. Now! Get out!' Her voice came back and shouted the command. 'Fuck off. I don't want you here!'

Vic hesitated but pulled on his leather jacket. 'Okay, okay, I didn't expect you to be so shitty. What's your problem? Can I at least dial a cab?'

She nodded, not looking at him. Rage boiled through her veins.

'Maybe you'll cheer up,' he sneered, pouring himself some vodka, 'and we can have a repeat performance.'

Lucy stared at the carpet, not thinking, scarcely breathing. She didn't change position until he slammed the door behind him.

Collapsing into a sob, she stretched out for the phone and pressed redial. Susan answered immediately.

'Lucy, how did it go? Isn't he still there?'

'Suse, I need your help.' She began to cry too much to speak.

'Lucy, what is it? Lucy?'

'I'll… I'll need to see the doctor tomorrow to sort something out. Something urgent. Will you come with me? Can you manage that?'

'I could. I can arrange things, but what is wrong?'

'I can't tell you much now. Please, just get here by 10.30 if you can.' Lucy felt a wave building to burst. 'I wasn't careful. I need to get sorted out. To make sure I'm not pregnant.'

Susan's shock reverberated in the silence. 'This was with Vic? What are you saying?'

'I can't talk about it now. Please, Suse, please just be here tomorrow.' Her words dribbled with tears. She needed to get to the bathroom, to deal with the laborious business of cleaning herself up; of trying to scrub away his revolting smell and the imprint that still weighed on her flesh.

'Luce, I'm worried now. I am. Is anyone with you? An assistant? And can't you ring your mum?'

Lucy almost laughed. 'I've been a bit lax in the dutiful daughter department. She wouldn't welcome me ringing now, blubbing for help to have my bum wiped. And worse.'

'No, she'd be okay, wouldn't she? She'd understand. I really think you shouldn't be on your own.'

'I need to be on my own, really,' she lied, smothering the tremor in her voice. 'Clear up my own mess and all that, a good little crip, independent to the last.'

'Now you sound *really* dreadful. Maybe I should try and come round.'

'No, no, I'm okay, please, Susan.' She felt desperation dragging her into the darkness of guilt. 'Suse, just be here for the doctor thing. Please. I appreciate the offer but… but I need to get washed up and into bed as soon as possible.'

'Why don't I pick up the morning-after pill? We'll talk about the doctor when I get there,' Susan said. 'Something else is very wrong. I know you. I know that wobble in your voice.'

Lucy said her goodbyes quickly. Wondering what she should do first, she attempted to move. Her legs were jelly, she was raw, deep into her vagina, so she gave up quickly. The phone sat nearby, still a friend. She began to dial, then saw her mother's startled face, and put it down with a sob. Eventually she wrenched herself into the bathroom and washed as best she could, but later, laying cold inside the sheets, the smell of his assault lingered.

For some time she lay still, calling her cat. She wanted to talk, impulsively tugging the phone onto her bed, dialling Russell's number. After three rings he answered but she slammed it down. The phone rang immediately and she listened to the low, tight pattern of his voice demanding that she pick up the phone.

It almost made her smile.

Thursday

Ringing in sick at 9.30, Terry answered her desk phone.

'Johnny boy won't mind. Nothing serious is it?' His voice came from a distance, clipped with wariness.

'No, just a bit under the weather. I'm going to the doctor's later.' Lucy spoke into the speaker phone, staring at her face in the mirror, dabbing at the scratches on her cheek and others that were unexpected.

'Okay then. Lucy, look, can we talk again? It's all been a bit of a head fuck, actually–'

'Yes, of course. We'll talk. Not now, though. When I'm back.' She tried to sound friendly, but she was tired. Very tired.

Susan arrived at 10.30 sharp, immediately full of questions. Lucy stuttered in avoidance, aching and full of sickness as she gulped down the pill presented to her. They left quickly for the surgery in Susan's car, with her assistant Sonia behind the wheel. The day was heavy, pushing into Lucy's head, and the unforgiving pain stayed raw between her legs.

Lucy mumbled out to the receptionist that her need was urgent.

After an hour she was speaking to a new white-haired doctor.

'I'm worried I might be pregnant. I took the morning-after pill earlier. And my face… they're other things too.' She waved her hands, unable to give him detail.

'Pregnant? What do you mean?' The doctor spoke over her.

Susan's sigh was loud. Lucy shivered and lowered her head. 'I had unprotected sex last night. An accident. And things got… difficult.'

Frowning, he held a fat, glinting fountain pen over her notes. She stared at it, watching as the doctor scratched down a comment. He asked what her long-term medical *complaint* was and nodded. 'Well, the morning-after pill isn't a sweetie, my dear. And in your case, you've taken risks by doing that.'

Lucy felt tears stinging into the scratches on her face. 'But can you check me over now? Do something? Examine my vagina?'

The doctor waved his pen like a baton. 'I really feel it best to wait. Wait until your next period. Whatever else, there should be a termination.'

Susan spoke up. 'You're not really taking Lucy seriously. Disabled women do have sex, you know. Why can't you treat her the same as anyone else in this situation?'

The doctor coughed and stared at Lucy's notes. 'I have listened to Ms. Hicks and treated this matter with the utmost seriousness. I see no reason for immediate concern. We will deal with matters as and when they arise.'

He looked at Lucy with dull and unmoved eyes. Everything in his tone muttered disbelief that she had had sex *at all.* Lucy could sense it and shook with the overwhelming need to go home.

*

After Sonia brought them back, Lucy saw at once the red eye of the answer phone, winking that she had more messages. She wondered if one was from Russell. It was almost a week since he had broken that particular promise.

'Come on, Luce. No more holding back,' Susan demanded. 'That was terrible at the GP. Start at the beginning. I know there's more to it than Vic. What happened? Did he assume you were on the pill or what? Did you forget and fall into a frenzy?'

Lucy looked away. 'No. Look, first I want to explain something. I don't know how it all happened, but it did. I've been with a guy, over the last six days. Someone different, I mean, each night. Not exactly planned, and as for *last* night–'

She began to sob.

'Ah,' Susan said, and gazed at the cat which trotted into the room.

'Don't look like that,' said Lucy. 'Let's say, mostly I didn't hate it. It's been such a buzz.'

Susan toyed with one of the biscuits Helga had left on the table. 'So what went wrong? Vic did that to your face?'

Exhaustion dried her tears to sand. She had no more energy to waste on crying. 'Vic… he… well, I don't know what to say. You know we were going to the cinema?'

'He raped you, didn't he?' Susan whispered. 'That fucker raped you.'

Lucy looked at the window. The weather was so changeable, she could almost wish for snow, which would smooth everything out to a wonderful calm. Even while it would make it unsafe to go out.

'I don't know. Really. I feel confused. When it came to it, I didn't really want him.' Her eyes turned to find the cat and she rubbed a hand across her face.

'Well, what are you going to do about it? Luce, look at me. What are you going to do?'

Lucy lifted her head. 'I want to sit in my shower until I feel squeaky-clean. I won't let that bastard fuck me up. I won't. I'll bite the bullet with the rest.'

'I am shocked. I don't know what else to say. You should go to the police,' Susan said, voice shrill.

Lucy grimaced and shook her head. 'I can't face that. I'll deal with it whatever way I have to. But not that.'

Susan frowned, narrowing her eyes. 'Luce, I want to understand all this. You haven't really explained about these other men. One must be Tom but, all obvious things aside, why, Lucy? Why?'

'Because I wanted to. I wanted them. And I don't care what people might think. Whatever nice little names there are for women doing this sort of thing.'

'What, casual sex? *That* sort of thing?' Susan kept staring at the cat, which sat down and started to clean its paws.

'You disapprove, I can tell.' Misery clenched in Lucy's throat. 'But until last night, I chose to do it. And even with Vic. I don't know anymore. I invited him over, we kissed. I felt turned on by that, so what did I expect?'

'For fuck's sake! Whatever else, this fuck fest has done your brain in. No is no. Look at your face! If you'd had twenty men in the previous week, it doesn't make any difference.'

Susan paused and Lucy drank some tea. The sickness eased and she made herself smile. 'Well, six on the trot is nothing, is it, compared to what the normals get up to?'

Susan laughed humourlessly. 'What have you been reading? Do you really care what bloody so-called normal women are supposed to be doing? Are you in competition? Do you feel happy now you've done it?'

'Fucking hell, Suse, if one more person mentions happy, I'll scream.'

'Okay, okay. So why, really. If it's not a stupid question to such an innocent, celibate creature as moi?'

'Because I could,' Lucy cried, surprised at her own answer. 'I needed to.'

'Why? You don't look that brilliant on it.'

'Haven't you ever wanted to do something, I don't know – something dangerous? Something against the so-called rules?' Heat bloomed in her cheeks as she dragged the words out. 'It's something *we're* not supposed to do. I mean women, and disabled women especially. I suppose it's like a kind of freedom. I wanted to do it, so I did.'

'But you're bloody miserable. I know you are, Luce,' Susan shook her head. 'I'm not going to get all moral on you. It's not about morals. But what can I say?'

Lucy finished her tea. The tabby cat returned and curled up on the sofa. But Lucy felt threatened by the new winds that shook the last autumn leaves from the shivering trees in the street outside.

'This week has been a bit over the top, I admit that. But it's hard to stop.' Lucy laughed ruefully. 'It kind of feeds itself.'

'But we can't win, you know,' Susan retorted. 'Men are hypocrites. Maybe we are too. The double standards are still there.'

'Oh Suse, you've been fantastic.' Lucy spoke slowly, toying with her cup, not sure what to say. 'A treasure of a mate. I couldn't have made it through this morning without you. But I can't do anything about Vic. Not in the obvious sense.'

She stroked Stripy, who had climbed closer for attention.

'One idea. Ring your mum,' Susan said. 'Tell her whatever you want, but ring her.'

Lucy smiled. 'I'll try. I know I should.'

And when she did, there was no answer, and the answer machine did not click on.

*

Relaxed into the bed, with fresh clean sheets, Lucy listened as rain played soothing rhythms on the windows.

'Stripy, puss-puss,' she cooed, and the cat came at once, landing on the bed with a pleased chirrup. 'Just us tonight, Baby. Just you to keep me warm. None of that frantic stuff.'

Becoming drowsy, listening to the rain, a ribbon of thought meandered. The answer machine revealed only a backlog of mostly boring messages. Suddenly she cried out, making the cat jump off the bed. 'You bastard, why, why didn't you ring? Russell, why?'

She knew she must cry at last, for him, and for herself.

Lava Lamp

As wandering gulls splashed white in the high summer sky, Ellen breathed in a mixture of marshland and dusty pollution. Catching the Docklands Light Railway from the grim station at Woolwich Arsenal, she made an effort to stop grinning at the little train leaning into the curve as it swung over the industrial sprawl below. She gazed down as it arched up along the toy-town track, wondering about the people who worked in the grey buildings, glad she was not one of them.

Sliding slowly into London with several old ladies and one isolated shaven-headed kid who skulked on at Poplar, she ignored the variety of their stares and shifted her gaze between Keith, who sat opposite, and the increasingly built-up landscape.

Keith tapped his foot. Tap, tap, tap, a slow turgid beat. Ellen switched back to stare through the window at the growing procession of ugly buildings.

'I hope this idea with Adam is going to work out okay. It could be a total disaster. We don't know him that well now, not really.' Keith snatched her attention, speaking too loudly.

She laughed, a hard noise jumping from a corner in her head. 'You're the one that set it all up. It'll change our routine a bit, obviously. But that could be good for us.'

He still tapped, pulling a questioning face.

'What?' Ellen shrugged. 'Stop. It's giving me a headache.'

The floor of the carriage rocked. Outside the sky remained harsh and rigid with heat.

She distracted herself with thoughts of her latest craft project. The decorative tiles were coming along, they sold well at local craft fairs and she felt she could try a new colour range. Slowly the thoughts trailed to re-runs of an argument she'd had with Keith, when he told her to give it up as a waste of time.

Or that she must do it 'properly', which, to him, meant making big money.

The rumbling rush down into the station at Bank was a giddy dive into a sudden stifling hell. As the train came to a stop, swarms of people clamoured. There was shouting and laughing, and kids wailing over the endless shrill of trains. At the platform, Ellen pushed forward as best she could, pressing firmly on her crutches, ignoring the eyes of tourists, who always stared without restraint.

As she waited with Keith, she gulped in air that felt too hot to breathe. Dust hit her throat and they didn't speak but hung back at the agreed meeting point until, eventually, the tall slim figure they were expecting came grinning out of the mass.

Adam, the permanent student. Young Adam, as Keith always called him, although he was now past 21. She remembered posting the birthday card. But whether that was one year ago, three, or maybe a little more, she could not, for the moment, remember. She *did* recall the striking postcard of moonlit pyramids he sent for her 30th.

As Adam approached, and Ellen registered his

arrival, she was consumed by the actuality of him, and his imminent stay. Here was a beautiful, striking, masculine adult.

'Ellen, hi, how are you?' He grinned, swaying on his feet, hands flitting and nervous. She detected a trace odour of fresh sweat and managed not to jump as he leant to peck her cheek.

Adam shook Keith's hand as another train arrived from another line. The main lift was a hideous crush of jostling travellers. It would be hard to negotiate and she was careful as she inched forward. Adam offered his arm, reading her mind better than Keith did. Not rough and not rude and unthinking. Immediately she took hold of him, shivering to link against his warm, tanned skin.

Keith's smile sagged. She knew he was drifting to thoughts of business, the mysteries of insurance, and the worry that he had taken a day off from those joys, and the allure of ever-changing secretaries. The dreadful pulse in her temples grew stronger, and as they finally moved out of the station, a dirty London breeze tangled her hair.

Drenched in the noise of Lombard Street, they moved along to a café on the corner of King William Street. Keith dashed inside without a word. Ellen knew he would order three cappuccinos and they would accept them gratefully.

Adam laughed, shifting on his heels. 'We could go off now, in a cab, me and you, Ellie,' he grinned. 'Play a trick on ol' Keithy boy. Imagine his face!'

Ellen tried to reply over the sound of double-decker buses snarling through the clogged junction. Adam scrunched his face up to signal he couldn't hear. Shrugging, she gave up, steadying her breath.

A few brief notes exchanged in the past. That was all she had of him. Snatches of news on postcards coming from endless unexpected locations. She had never stopped to think much about him other than as a growing teenager. As Keith's relation.

Now he was undeniably a man, holding her arm, scanning her face intently.

'Ellie,' he began as the traffic held its breath, 'no wheelchair this time?'

A needle pricked. Was she to be forever filed away by her wheelchair? She pushed the needle away. This was Adam asking a simple question. Not a nosing relative always prepared for her miracle cure.

'I lost it at Limehouse Station,' she joked quickly. 'It sort of rolled off when I wasn't looking. Or maybe a skinhead nicked it.'

'Oh, tease,' he laughed, pulling a face in apology.

Ellen wanted to have his mouth on hers, there, then, amidst the bustle of the London street. The thought hijacked her. She paused and answered at the next appropriate gap in the growl of the traffic.

'You know how it goes, Adam. A wheelchair is only a thing, a useful thing that helps me get around when I need it, and today I didn't feel like I did.'

'Okay,' he replied with a nod, as the noise swelled again, stopping their conversation. Gently letting go of her arm, he walked a few steps away, hands fidgeting in pockets, his hair black-brown, a wriggle of thick strings.

As the London air pressed her down, she noticed his clothes. Jeans tight around his lean shape and a short-sleeved pale green shirt, open a little at the neck. She turned away, knowing she was staring.

They sipped at their too-hot drinks, watching pigeons peck at random rubbish. After throwing the half-full cups in a bin, Keith stood at the kerb to hail a black cab while Adam stayed beside her.

'We're being taken to Covent Garden for a posh lunch,' Ellen informed him when the din died down, 'before Keith is drawn back to the wonders of insurance.'

'You'll be around though, won't you?' Adam asked, guardedly. 'To keep me happy and entertained?'

'Yes, I'll look after you.' Ellen shouted to make sure he heard, aware that her hands were sweating and her crutches had started to rub the flesh at the back of her elbows. As they waited for the cab, she put more effort into holding his solid arm.

Sweet, friendly Adam, all grown up.

Adam, a man.

A man she wanted to believe that she could have.

*

The long days of summer melted past. Returning from a city meander, Adam panted into the room. At her work table, Ellen attempted to paint tiles, fighting against the thickening glaze.

'Well?' He stood in the doorway, grinning. 'My hair, Ellie.'

She was in the lounge, a large square room with open French windows that led onto a wide patio. The breeze brought in the smell of honeysuckle. She wiped her paint-spattered fingers on a cloth with laborious, deliberate movements. The light from a beloved lava lamp shed a soft glow around them, turning Adam into a big grey shadow as he dipped quickly down beside her.

'Give it a pat then, go on,' he encouraged softly. 'It feels weird.'

Ellen put one hand on his head, trying not to shake. His hair was smooth and velvet. As she leant forward, his thighs brushed her knees. She was glad Keith was staying late at the office again.

Her palms sang as she caressed through his hair. He didn't move away, but closed his eyes and twisted his head to follow her hand. His warm body jostled and tantalised casually against her. Stopping abruptly, she picked up her paintbrush. He sank back onto the floor, smiling, eyes glowing in the subdued light.

'Does it ever, umm, bother you?' He explained himself by turning to look at her crutches nearby. 'Over the years I've never really asked you. I wasn't sure how to.'

'A pair of crutches, a wheelchair, you know, like I've said before – so what? They're just basically helpful things, Adam. Only hateful when others use them to give me labels. This body of mine, it's not such a problem, really. It's my body.'

'You don't mind me asking, do you?' His voice was soft as he ran his fingers over the plain blue rug beneath him.

'I am horribly outraged and disturbed,' she joked. This was safe ground, talking about her and her disability, just as everyone expected. Usually the assumption made her peevish, and she loathed being constrained into clichés about medical conditions, disparaged with ideas of what a disabled person was. 'Other people bother me. Assume they know about my life.' She paused, then found herself continuing quickly. 'Does my disability ever bother you? People do stare and all that. You must have noticed.'

He looked hard into her eyes. She held her breath until he smiled.

'You don't really think it would, do you? I've never thought of you as some cripple, if that's what you mean,' he said at last.

'Not a cripple, Adam? I must get around to educating you in the language of disability. But I'm disappointed. I must be doing something totally wrong if I'm obviously boring Mrs Wifey of ol' Keithy boy.'

'Oh, no. I don't mean that,' he muttered, moving closer. 'You're, um–'

He hesitated and shook his head. She realised he had moved close enough for
her to touch him again and somehow her hand was on his arm. As she flinched back he pretended not to notice.

'You're Ellie. You're family. You're cool. No worries,' he laughed at last, squeezing her fingers.

She blanked out what urged her down a dangerous path and stared very hard at the lava lamp.

'I love your hair, Adam. Very practical. What should I say, to stop you thinking I'm a total old fossil?' The words strained out, ordinary and opaque, but her mouth stayed cramped with secrets.

Adam stood up in a big movement, a typically enigmatic smile passing over his face.

'I've had a great idea, Ellie. You and me are going out. We are going on a bus trip.'

She had to laugh. 'We are, are we? Bet you haven't travelled about much like that with a disabled person before.'

He waved a dismissive hand. 'Don't talk bollocks. The weather is fantastic and you've been stuck indoors working on those tiles for ages. Isn't London the most accessible city in the world with its buses?'

'Yes, but it can be a farce. Lots of hassles.' She resisted without conviction. She wanted to go, of course. She wanted to spend a day out with Adam. With *this man*. Despite the fear, the practicalities. The threat of the bus ramps breaking down, the horror of never finding a decent accessible toilet. How could she tell him about those things?

'Don't be arsey,' he persisted. 'It'll be fun.'

She knew there was nothing else to say.

He scooted off, shouting, 'Ciao,' as he left the house.

*

Ellen noticed a dead wasp, curled and crisp in her bedroom window as she pulled the cord to close the curtains. Keith hovered behind her, his hands heavy on her shoulders. It was obvious he had been drinking.

'You're still my princess, aren't you?' he breathed into her hair, pressing his weight against her.

Ellen shook him away, deflating beneath him. 'I'm tired, Keith. I need a good night's sleep.'

'Not before a bit of love and affection, my dear, surely?' he tried to coo, jabbing a finger over her neck, underneath her hair. 'Tuesday's normally our day, isn't it?'

Ellen slowly sat on the bed, her back to him. Tears burnt from her eyes.

'Keith no, please, I'm too tired.'

He sagged onto his side of the bed and said nothing, but shoved himself under the sheet, sighing heavily.

'Don't. I won't play that game.'

'Who's playing any game?' he snapped at her back. 'I don't think you really fancy me anymore.'

Ellen pulled her mouth together. She stared at the windowsill, wondering how the wasp had died.

*

The sun stayed high with the morning, full of birdsong and the smell of open flowers floating on the breeze. Ellen sat in the kitchen with Adam, the remains of Keith's meal the only sign of his earlier presence at home. Kate, the personal assistant working the morning slot, cleared away the breakfast things.

'Have I ever really explained about PAs, Adam? You've seen Kate,' Ellen said. 'They're people we choose and control ourselves. Lots of disabled people have PAs now, rather than old-fashioned carers.'

He absorbed each answer with a smile and a narrowing of his eyes. 'Yeah-yeah, of course I know. Disabled friends at university have them, Ellie. I know about PAs. Thought about going for the job once with this guy. Never got around to it.'

Surprised, she hid her face in her mug of tea. How things had changed since she was in her twenties.

'We'll take the 101 from Wanstead High Street around the corner,' Adam announced, putting down the list of accessible buses. 'Seems the easiest.'

'Oh nice,' Kate grimaced and rolled her eyes. 'The route into the total arse end of London.'

'Watch it, you,' Ellen chided but Kate's sarcasm

was soothing. 'It's up to Adam. He's organised this trip.'

'Yep, absolutely. Now, I've got to grab a few things from my room, take a pee, then we'll be off if you're ready.' He stuffed his iPhone into his ubiquitous rucksack and flew into the hall.

'I've got to strain my bladder dry,' Ellen muttered at Kate. 'I can hardly ask Adam to help me in a crappy bog, can I?'

'Maybe not but you should go for it, Ellie,' Kate leered towards her immediately. 'Give him a sign you're up for something.'

'What?' Ellen choked and almost spilled her tea.

'Come off it, Ell. I've worked here for too long. You're looking different. I see your eyes light up when he looks at you.'

'It's not so fucking obvious, is it? I know I'm being totally pathetic.'

'Why is it pathetic?' Kate looked at her with steely eyes. 'You're not getting stuck in the usual "I'm not good enough" shit, are you? I'm telling you, Adam has thoughts about you that aren't the sort you have for maiden aunts.'

'Has he said something?'

The question leapt out as Kate moved across the kitchen to peer around the door. 'Look,' she said, 'he'll be back any minute. Just enjoy today. You know you want to be with him. Be brave.'

As Adam's fast footsteps approached, Ellen knew that Kate was right.

*

There was a brief wait at the bus stop alongside the

small park on Wanstead High Street. The large horse chestnut trees waved hello in the wind, their full branches offering welcome shade to the elderly, while young children squealed at squirrels arcing across the wide expanse of grass.

Ellen's chair was fully powered and she nagged to herself to remember that she was simply entertaining Adam, who was Keith's relative, staying for the summer.

She wore a yellow-gold cotton dress with an orange blouse over it and couldn't deny that she looked good. The low cut of the dress suited her full breasts, the colours complementing the tone of her skin.

When the ramp slid out of the 101, Adam didn't gush with amazement as even her seasoned workers sometimes did. He stood by, offering help only when requested. She was pleased to see the drop-down seat beside the wheelchair space was free, meaning they were able to sit together for the journey.

The bus was soon in East Ham, with its lively crowds and endless sari shops that she loved to frequent for craft items. The smell of spices enriched the air, as the bus, a slow grumbling beast soon crammed with restless passengers, pushed towards the river.

'How's uni going, then?' she asked.

'Okay I suppose,' he said, smoothing down his dark pelt of hair. 'Really shit sometimes, great at others. But I think I'm getting bored with it. Not sure if I should have gone on to do this MA.'

He smiled, and a rush charged through Ellen's guts. She looked out of the window.

'Are you all right?' His hand was over hers in a rapid movement. 'You look worried. I haven't bullied you too much today, have I? About coming out like this? I didn't mean to take it for granted that you would, you know.'

The bus approached its last stop at North Woolwich. In the heavy air and scorching sun, how could she tell Adam anything? 'I'm fine, really. I probably needed to get out. Keith's away so much these days.'

Adam snorted and shook his head. 'He's a funny bloke. How can he enjoy working so much? When he could be at home with you for at least some of the day.'

A chill stream crept into the warm air. 'Oh Adam, I'm not stupid. Promise not to say anything. Keith has other interests at work *besides* his job, if you get my meaning.'

'Oh,' he said, curling his lips inwards. 'I'm shocked because, well, apart from anything, it's like you don't really care.'

'I don't. We weren't a big love-match. I never pretended. Keith knows that.'

Ellen sensed his disapproval and they fell into silence until they were out on the roadside, waiting for the ferry to dock.

'What about you? Would he be shocked if–' Adam let the sentence trail into the warm air before continuing. 'Would he be shocked if you did the same?'

Ellen stared into the river, watching its calming motion and the brilliance of light sprinkled on its surface. 'I expect so, but only because I'm his. He married me and I belong to him. That's just how he thinks. It's all so clear; so neat and tidy. But he's not such a bad man. Really, he's not.'

Adam looked at her again without a smile, eyes

glittering in the sun.

'Anyway, I don't want to talk about Keith. You're all mine today. Look, we can cross.'

She couldn't hold his gaze and pushed the control of her wheelchair forward to take her quickly onto the ferry.

*

The smiling sun followed them as they meandered through the insalubrious market and the colourless roads around it. They shared lunch at a cheap and cheerful greasy spoon and perused second-hand books in charity shops.

Ellen noticed a 'disabled toilet' sign pointing down an uninspiring street, and hesitated. Could she ask him to help? If she went to check it out – and it was a disaster – he would then know she wanted to use it. She could imagine it would reek, the floor would be sticky with endless sprays of urine – and there might be used needles in the sink. All this to consider before deciding whether it was the right height and size, with enough bars to use it for what it was meant.

She could not do it, and made a firm note to herself to avoid drinking anything else. The half-can of soda would have to do.

'You've certainly seen some grimy London outskirts today,' she said, laughing as they returned to the ferry for the homeward journey.

'No, it's been great. Something a bit different. We'll do it again soon.'

She decided to stand up for the return crossing on the ferry, to feel its subtle sway across the river directly through her body. Adam, tall beside her, quickly bent down to her level, leaning on the rail. 'Yeah, a great day,' he said, taking in a huge breath as the air filled with a cool wind that skimmed off the water.

Then, he kissed her cheek. Maybe she jumped. Unexpectedly, he remained so close to her face she could feel his breath. His mouth was almost there, asking for hers.

Ellen turned away. Seagulls swooped across the expanse, noisy and playful.

Later that night, she sobbed silently until her eyes were on fire.

*

Days sweltered and summer entered through the pores of Ellen's skin every time Adam looked at her. Finding herself in the kitchen with Keith one morning, he sulked that she was too quiet, claiming that something had changed; that she was different.

As Ellen stared at him, memories cut their way out of her head into the white harsh slabs of sun lying on the kitchen floor. Keith had been good to her. He had made her life easier than it could have been. But Adam made her wonder.

She looked up to push these useless thoughts away, and Keith turned his sour face towards her. 'I won't be home till late. Might be better if I leave it and just stay in a hotel again.'

The sentence trailed off into the feeble steam of her tea.

'Sure,' Ellen said, and gave her toast a challenging stare. She knew what he'd be doing, and she didn't care.

'Adam's around.' Keith grimaced the statement into her face, annihilating the remains of his breakfast. 'He'll be here to keep you company, won't he?'

'I suppose so,' she said, hating him for tossing Adam's name into the stiff air, picking it from her thoughts like a shameful scab torn open.

'What? What's that face for?' His lips were white as he spat out his impatience on tiny flecks of wet toast.

'I'll be happier when he's gone home.' The words burnt on her tongue.

'What is the matter with you? This visit has been settled for ages. Maybe you're run-down.' He smiled indulgently. 'Adam's been no trouble, has he? I know you've had some good days out. He likes you, I keep telling you not to worry.'

She said nothing. It would be better if Adam did go home. Home to the safe regions of the past.

*

A day arrived when the summer's merciless pulse dampened Adam's delight with the city. A day when Keith phoned in to say he would be away for the night, again.

Ellen took Kate through the preparation of dinner, which they ate between bitty, subdued conversation.

Adam seemed preoccupied too, while Ellen fixed her thoughts on the innocent intricacies of planning colours for the next run of tiles. As she gave Kate instructions to clear away the dinner things, she tried to ignore the background sounds of Adam ambling around the flat.

'You'll have your chance tonight, Ellie,' Kate whispered, simultaneously pushing the door to almost shut it. 'Remember, Keith isn't a saint. So don't you live to regret what you haven't done.'

'What are you talking about?'

'Adam stayed in. He knows Keith's away,' Kate said, waving her hands.

'Stop it, you bugger! You're terrible.' Ellen made herself grin as Kate finished her tasks and prepared for the end of her shift.

Once she had left, Ellen's heart shrivelled to stone. She went into the lounge and sat down carefully beside Adam on the long, firm sofa where he was slumped, reading a novel.

'Kate's great,' he said, not lifting his eyes. They talked, easy slow chat. She explained her ideas for designs, about glazes, how unpredictable they were, the mess she got in. They laughed together.

Inside her, summer sweated some more.

The days kept long, and light tapered off slowly into a heavy sunset where the blue sky gave in unwillingly to night. She picked up a book when their conversation reached a natural lull, relishing Adam's presence which rolled over her like a balm.

'Do you want a light on, Ellie?' he asked softly. 'Hey, nice lava lamp. I've never really noticed it before. Can we put that on for a while?'

She nodded and dropped her gaze to it on the table beside her. 'It's not original '60s, though. Wish it was.'

She didn't mention that Keith had bought it, finding that she'd rather not bring up his name.

Adam crouched down to find the click-switch which was behind her feet. As he fumbled in the soft darkness, she closed her eyes and trembled in a kind of madness. Adam reached forward on his knees, and as he traced the lead back up to the lamp, he scrambled with his other hand to find the arm of the sofa. His fingers found her calf and she flinched.

Maybe he heard her breath. He didn't take his hand away but his other joined it, pushing back her skirt into ridges onto her thighs.

'Ellie,' he said. 'Ellie.'

The lava lamp glimmered hot thick red that stirred into the golden liquid. His hands went under her skirt, fingers edging into her knickers, probing into her damp pubic hair.

Ellen gasped and put her small hands over his, straining towards his caresses.

Suddenly, he leant his body over her, urging her down with tight whispers, down, down, onto the long, helpful sofa.

He found her mouth. Took it, gorged on the juice of it. She climbed between his moist lips and lapped at the need on his tongue. He pulled away, putting his legs on each side of her thighs.

'Ellie,' he muttered, leaning forward, kissing her, kissing everywhere, anywhere. 'Tell me… what you need me to do. I won't hurt you.'

Ellen wanted to sing aloud.

'I'm not a porcelain doll, Adam. I'm real, don't worry. I'll guide you.' She sighed, putting her hands on his face. 'And I've wanted this like stupid, for so long.'

'Yes, Ellie,' he grinned, then was back on her mouth, his tongue dancing a violent circle around hers.

Hands pushed away her clothes in big urgent movements, unveiling her, unwrapping her breasts, exposing her nipples to be covered by his lips, sucked to hard buds and raked by his tender teeth. Ellen muttered fast clear instructions to him. He helped to push a cushion under her buttocks then leant over her again. She felt his cock urging out for her. He moved quickly, with care, and tugged down the zip on his worn black jeans.

The room was now darker as the lava lamp shot up globules of fiery crimson, strange foetal forms growing in a golden amniotic fluid.

Ellen guided him to grasp one of her thighs firmly to support her.

She was jumbled up with Adam. He was everywhere on her, around her, and ran his hand between her legs, found her again, caressed into the juices that ached from her cunt. She squirmed against the delving of his confident fingers and murmured more instructions, guiding him to how she wanted it.

His cock entered her as she had dreamed, with no fuss or hesitation. She let out a caw of shivering cries, urging him to gorge in and out of her. Her orgasm spiralled – he was deep inside, pushing, pushing swiftly in a growling rhythm. His fingers stayed steady around her thighs as he held them. She savoured the sweet pain as he moved, coming quickly with a groan of release.

They were swallowed whole and melted into the drool of warning red that the lava lamp oozed around the room. As they gripped each other through every tremor, she was distantly aware that something brushed her skin which was caught on her foot.

She moved on reflex. At once, the lava lamp slid and toppled on its side with a heavy clunk.

It broke into its component pieces and the glass tube rolled to the table's edge. The soft luminescence swirled into a bloody stew and the room swam in a disapproving red-glow.

'Shit.' Adam jolted away to stop it falling, recklessly and hideously separating the slick joining of their flesh. He picked up the lamp tentatively and set it back in place.

Everywhere was sudden darkness, apart from the one blur of suffused light. Ellen turned her head away from the rolling colours.

Adam didn't speak but moved to the door, taking decisive steps away from her as he tidied his clothes.

'Shit, I'm sorry. Really sorry.'

'Adam?' Her voice was a reluctant whisper.

He left the room and she had no words to call him back, alone with the lava lamp as it oozed down to its sedate flux and flow. A sad wetness chilled her thighs.

Now there was the unthinkable. Now there was an after – which had not been contemplated; not mulled to pieces and chewed on from all angles. But she knew that from this night, she would not – could not – be as she was.

*

The next morning, Adam didn't join her, but she was tormented by hearing him in his room. Kate was there making breakfast but kept a tactful silence. Ellen felt sick and took nervous gulps of weak tea. New questions chased out the old. Prosaic, awkward fears, aware now of the risk she had taken with Adam – when she never once allowed herself the risks of unsafe sex with Keith (he hadn't bought her to that extent).

She bit her lip, unable to eat.

Eventually, Adam came into the kitchen. At first he stared at her, then smiled his usual grin while Kate left on the pretext of tidying the lounge.

'I've got to go, Ellie,' he said, lowering his eyes. 'I think it's for the best.'

She continued to drown in the dirty sea of betrayal. What would she tell Keith? It mattered more now it was real, not a fantasy that could accommodate itself in her head. She knew she could not blurt it out to Keith as a casual thing. Because it wasn't.

Adam slumped into new silence. When she looked at him, tall and desirable, she realised that the torment would start, and she guessed that she loved him, on this morning with the sun pouring into the kitchen.

As he left, moving to the door with less of his usual energy, she got a hint of an answer. She perched on the telephone seat in the hall, muttering inanities that he must send a postcard, must keep well.

'Ellie, don't.' His eyes were full and anxious as he put his hand on her face.

He kissed her goodbye.

Not a chaste kiss. Not a kiss for family. His mouth impelling her to open again to his hunger as it harmonised with her own.

But he left her. On the doorstep, weeping, desperate. Crushed back into a dead way of life she did not want. And perhaps, never really did.

*

A week later a parcel was sent to her. Another lava lamp. From Adam. The card with it said:

Dear Ellie,

I hope your lamp isn't broken. Put this one on and think of me. Maybe I can visit again soon? Please.

Adam.

She ripped the message to pieces before Keith saw it, her fingers wet as they rubbed out impossible tears.

Later, alone in the evening, she gazed at the new lamp which glowed mournfully pink, and contemplated the wavering embryos that floated inside their tiny restrained sea of sad pale blue.

Bound and Devoted

Bethany pulled her knees together, testing the restraints. There wasn't much slack. A smile crept at the corners of her mouth, though she kept her head down. Adrian wouldn't want her to smile and she would be punished if she moved too much. The pleasure of the punishment would come later, that was a relish to be drawn out.

The blindfold was arbitrary. A silk scarf over her eyes for theatrical effect. She could see him moving in the dim light ahead of her. He was taking off his prosthetic limb. Her stomach clenched and she licked her dry lips.

The leather straps tying her arms to her wheelchair were tight and her elbows were threatening to spasm. Even this made her slick between her legs. She was his very special pet, his toy, and cruelty never stretched to permanent damage, otherwise playing was restricted. After all, who would break their favourite toy?

He was coming closer, holding the furniture for support. Hovering directly in front of her, he pushed the stump of his leg between her knees and rubbed it hard against her exposed cunt.

She gasped, sighing with pleasure and the thrill of obscure fear.

*

They'd met at the swimming pool. Not any old swimming pool, but at a private members' health club in Islington. Bethany felt out of place, cadging guest passes for the pool – part of a gym otherwise inaccessible to her. Yet in the water she dissolved, floating and moving with delicious ease. Most sessions in the daytime were quiet, with the occasional rich old dear swimming a few lengths in her designer swimsuit.

Bethany liked that, so on the day she came into the pool to see Adrian slipping over the edge into the still waters, she scowled, waiting for the splashing and macho endurance swimming, accompanied with the usual grunts.

Seconds later she realised his leg was missing from above the knee. Her thoughts jumbled. There was always that ridiculous flush of kinship and curiosity. He was a crip, wasn't he? How did he see himself? Was he in the closet, playing it down, keen to pass as a Norm?

As her assistant helped her onto the hoist that winched her into the water, she felt a sudden sense of self-consciousness, wondering whether her pubes were showing. Had she smudged in the heat?

He did not look over at her, but swam, quiet and focused. As he turned after one length, she stared at the marvellous shape of his lean male body sliding through the water, his shorter limb in harmony with his movements.

Slipping into the warmth she looked away, the hoist lowered to maximum. Now she could move, stretch herself, and enjoy pushing her body.

As she went through her exercise routines, she made surreptitious glances in his direction. He remained stoic and silent, and she was too shy to introduce herself. Soon it was time to be hoisted out. Looking down, he caught her by surprise as she settled back into her wheelchair, wrapped in a white fluffy towel.

'Hi, I think I've met you,' he smiled, water running down his skin, as he steadied himself expertly with the wall.

She noticed his nipples were bullets in the cold and felt the blush as she smiled and looked away. 'Don't think so.'

'You go to demos, don't you? I talked to you once at an anti-cuts rally. You dropped your banner and I picked it up.'

Bethany grinned. 'Oh. I remember now. You look different.'

'I was wearing rather more clothes then. A lot more. It was February, wasn't it?'

'Yes, February. One of the first actions. It was cold. And remember the police kettled us?'

'Stupid that was.' He shook his head, looking at her hard. 'I'm Adrian, by the way. And you are… Bethany.'

'I'm embarrassed now, I didn't remember your name.' She fussed with her towel which had dropped down to reveal a scar along the outside of her hip and thigh. As she pulled it up, she blushed harder to see him staring at it.

'I'm freezing my tits off here. Fancy sharing a coffee in the members' lounge after?' He leaned his backside against the wall, grabbing a towel and wash bag.

Bethany noticed the brilliant blue of his eyes and stammered. This was not what happened to her. She was invisible and mostly happy with that. Only sometimes did she yearn for more, and then it was hard to find it, or to even pin down what it was.

'OK, yes, why not?' Her voice trembled. Licking her lips, she tried to calm herself.

'Great.' Adrian winked and turned to leave.

Bethany noticed that in his movement, he stared again, eyes narrowed at her long snaky scar.

*

Everything rushed forward fast from that point. They went to dinner, they went to meetings about demos, they did the demos, and they snuggled on her sofa. Adrian told her about his impairment that night. He'd lost his leg in the army, not being a hero, but from an accident during a training exercise. Now he worked for the local authority as a park's attendant. He also had a disabled sister.

'She helped me a lot after the accident. Though she can be a pain sometimes. She always knows better. Gets patronising,' he said in passing, as they met up again at the pool.

As Bethany let the water lap at her skin, she smiled at him. They hadn't fucked yet. Almost everything but penetration. She didn't want to complain, she was happy with his hands feathering lightly over her body, his tongue dancing magic on her clit. Yet it seemed strange, and she didn't know how to talk about it.

He did a few lengths, then came up to her, flicking water as he did, holding a square float.

'When you descend on that hoist I want to give you a drum roll. It looks very regal.'

'I *am* very regal,' she teased, kissing him quickly.

He surveyed the pool which was empty apart from them, and slipped under the lane divider to stand beside her.

'I want to treat you like a queen.' His voice was low, intense. 'Let me make you come, now in the pool.'

Bethany burnt red and squirmed.

'Adrian, no! We'll be caught.'

'We can make out we're exercising. You'll have to try and keep quiet though.' Leaning closer to her, he grinned, swaying his head. 'None of your delicious loud moaning. Say yes, please, say yes.'

She was already aroused. 'How? You can't exactly shove your hand in my costume here.'

'I won't use my hands, I'll do this.'

Suddenly he had put his stump between her legs and pulled her forward so pressure was exerted on her stirred clit. One hand moved to her hip and began to stroke the line of her scar, up and down.

'Oh…' she sighed, resting against him. 'Yes. Do it.'

Making one last sweep around the pool, he started to rock gently.

'All good exercise, Bethany, isn't it?' he said, eyes moving from her to watch the entrance hall.

Bethany knew she would come quickly. The sensation of freedom in the water, the frisson of being caught, and her unfair frustration at not having his cock made the urge rise like a fierce fire. Her limbs trembled as he kept up the steady pressure, the light stroking, the ripples of pleasure lifting from her centre, tightening her muscles, hijacking her in a burst of intense release.

'Yes, Adrian, yes,' she hissed, ramming herself on him, 'fuck me soon darling, please fuck me.'

The orgasm rolled through her, fading into warm waves.

He laughed and kissed her head. 'Soon, I promise. Soon. I need to tell you something first. This evening?'

'What? Is it naughty?' she said, regaining her breath, quite sure she was red from tip to toe, amazed she had done such a thing.

'It is naughty, and it is different.' He moved away, keeping his eyes steady, and his thoughts secret.

As she shook her head and moved towards the hoist, there in his tight black trunks she saw the enormous tormenting bulge of his cock. She swallowed, feeling a new hunger squirm between her legs.

*

The day was warm even with her back door open. She turned on the TV and flicked. Lots of Olympics. Runners were lining up for the 400 metres, hoping to qualify for the semis. Bethany yawned, checking her watch and looking up to see the cameras on Jonnie Peacock. The commentator enthused about his achievements, the first double amputee to compete in the 'main' Olympics, and the wonder of his 'cheetah' feet.

She grinned. He was like Adrian, only younger. Her eyes absorbed the athlete and his toned body, impatient for Adrian to arrive.

She sifted through piles of paper, clicked through emails, noting down dates for new demonstrations. How strange it felt to be in the firing line to lose her benefits. There were no jobs for an inexperienced English grad like her anyway – without the barriers, the prejudice, the insensitivity to her need for rest and pacing.

A bleep from her mobile phone caught her attention, wiping away concerns with work assessment tests and her uncertain future.

Not long now, darling. Bus full, nearly fell over. Big things to tell you! Axxxx

She read it with a pleased grin, intrigued, and quickly put away her folders. Planning their appearance at the next anti-cuts action could wait.

He was there at the door within five minutes, bounding in with a bottle of prosecco, glancing up at the TV as she opened the door.

He chatted, kissed her, pulled his boots off, removed his limb and nestled on the sofa.

'Speedy!' she said. 'Now, no teasing. Spit it out. What's the big thing?'

He hesitated and slipped his broad hand under her skirt, into the edge of her knickers to find the scar.

'I'm a devotee,' he said softly, the hand stroking and stroking. 'But don't be scared.'

Bethany giggled.

'My devotee?'

'Yes, and yes,' he whispered. 'But not exactly how you think. Don't you know your stuff? Have you never heard of a devotee in a disability context?'

'That sounds rather sociological.' She frowned, stopping his hand from moving along her thigh. 'What are you talking about?'

'OK, I'm going for broke. I love scars. Your scars. I've loved disabled women, especially with scars, even before my accident.'

Bethany froze. Jonnie Peacock was on the starting blocks, and the tension in the stadium radiated from her TV into the air around them.

'What?' Bethany edged herself up, stomach turning. 'Say that again.'

Adrian moved away, rubbing his eyes. He poured himself a full glass of wine.

'I can't believe you don't know. You must. It's not nasty or anything.'

Thoughts would not process. She couldn't form words for a response. She just blinked, mouth open.

Abruptly she swung herself into her wheelchair and was quickly at her computer. She typed in *disabled woman devotee* and thousands of sites rolled out of Google.

'Darling, it's okay, don't get all worked up. I'm crazy about you.'

'Or my scars?' She felt frosty and kept clicking.

The start gun went for the 400 metres and she couldn't help but look at the TV. Jonnie flew along, his blade a blur. The crowd roared.

Adrian came up behind her and kissed her neck. She didn't respond.

'I love *you*, Baby. I love Bethany. All of her.'

As the race finished to tumultuous applause, she sagged. He had never said it before, not at any time they'd been seeing each other. She knew he liked her scars, to stroke and lick them. But this was different.

'You must have something you like, a particular thing,' he whispered, nuzzling her again. 'What gives you a kick, darling?'

Her face raged red as memories poured into the frost and warmed her. Her ex-husband, Alan, and her initiation into the pleasures of bondage. At first, she had resisted, and protested in a conventional way. Then, relenting, she'd tried it to please him and found herself transformed with endless new sexual experiences and pleasures. It had been a long time.

'Adrian, I like bondage,' she blurted and grabbed his hand. 'I like being tied up, restrained and tormented to within an inch of my life. Then fucked. Senseless. Alan introduced me to it. I was collared and owned. I like to submit.'

She was hot with confusion and shame. Hypocrisy laughed in her head and pushed her to cry.

Adrian stood back to stare at her. Looking down at the floor, she wanted to dissolve into the TV and be swept away into the obscuring crowds. Now who was the big pervert?

As she tentatively lifted her head, she saw Adrian smiling, his eyes alive with pleasure.

'Beth, oh my darling. You sneaky, wonderful, sexy thing.'

He held onto her chair and lowered himself down. They fell into each other's arms, laughing and giggling.

*

The first time was exquisite. Adrian tied her hands together slowly and placed a blindfold over her eyes. He'd bought it especially, a black silk scarf. On the bed he helped her get on her side, showing off, he said, his favourite scar on her body. Her left hip, with its snake of hardened skin, pale now with age but a demarcation of her past, her experience.

When his tongue licked along the ridge of the scar, with slow deliberation, making a steady and tormenting way down, across and between the aching cleft of her thighs, she cried out.

He hushed her as he rolled her back a little to press deeper; to rub his lips into her pubic hair, to wheedle his tongue around her clit.

He stopped suddenly, and, leaving her panting but moving her back, gently edged himself between her legs. He moved his thigh against her, his shorter limb fitting there snugly.

In the darkness of her blindfold, she could smell him. She could hear his breath. Delicious tension heightened her desire, as the restraints were altered to let her arms fall to her sides before reattachment.

'You'll get what you want now, darling,' he breathed close to her face, rubbing against her in a steady rhythm.

The restraints were tightened hard and the blindfold ripped away. She saw him above her, his cock raging hard. He lowered himself and thrust.

At first, he did not move, and Bethany moaned gently, lost to the pleasure of clenching him, revelling in the sensation of his fullness inside her.

He moved, hard and deep, not fast. She pulled up against her ties, and he pushed her down.

She thought she would break with arousal.

As he quickened his pace, he allowed her to move with him. Occasionally, he stopped, tormenting her by pulling out, to blow on her clit, to rub his rigid cock between her lips.

Back inside her, he moved faster, but with control. She rippled and shook beneath him, wrestling against the restraints.

'Bethany,' he hissed on a deep thrust as she came, alight, exploding.

She looked up as he pulled out, directing his pulsing semen onto her scar, oiling it with the sticky white fluid, fingers rubbing gently its length. Her orgasm stretched on at this caress and she cried out again.

For a few more minutes he continued, then flopped down to hold her. They were still and quiet, curled into each other.

'Demo tomorrow then?' Bethany said suddenly, and they both laughed.

'Yes, yes, we're going,' he teased, then looked up at his leg against the wall, and grinned.

'Did you hear it by the way? Jonnie got gold.'

She laughed some more and kissed Adrian.

On the lips, and on his stump.

Nippy Days

First shared at the White Rabbit Story Collective

hand into my little bra and pulls at my own hardened nipple.

That was that. Addicted in one sweet moment, all those years ago. Yet why do so many men get all heated up when I show my unashamed interest in their sadly neglected little buds?

'Hey. Annie. Daydream girl.' Alex poked me with his ruler from the desk. 'You processed those invoices?'

I stared at Alex in his neat blue shirt.

'Yes. Almost,' I lied.

But really, I was recalling the last set of male nipples I'd seen.

Jim was buff. All over. He wore tight vests under casually worn shirts. He liked me enough to take me out for dinner. He was a boob man and that suits me. I yearned for the moment of mutual pinching. And maybe he would be the one to gasp, 'bite my nipple as I come'.

We bantered, as you do. I fizzed, hopeful, crossing and uncrossing my legs.

I invited him in for coffee. We sat on the sofa kissing, drinking. I found my hands urging hard under his clothes, as his fingers made busy with the buttons of my blouse.

The hairs along the centre of his chest invited my caress to reach higher.

I found my first target, a firm ridge of raised flesh. My stomach, and down, down below, my pussy clenched.

Alex jumped away as though I had shoved a hot poker in his nipple.

'Oh, no, don't,' he said, with a nervous laugh. 'That feels weird.'

'You don't like them being touched?' I trembled.

'Not really, if I'm honest.' He grinned. 'But there IS something else up for a firm grip.'

I sighed. I could have shrugged, laid back and thought of… nipples. No. I was too disappointed.

He went home, much confused. I lay on my bed feeling deflated, yet stirred from the expectation of a sexy adventure and a set of hot man nips.

My mind drifted. One evening at a burlesque show with friends I was stunned to see a guy appear on stage, complete with pasties on his nipples and a long cock tassel. For the uninitiated, pasties are nipple tassels, and twirling does not require a large female breast. It's all about bounce and this cute guy had plenty. My eyes were glued to those red sequined cones and I nearly fainted when he ripped them off for his finale, showing big fat hard manly nipples.

I thought about him and slid my hand into my knickers. I groaned as I dreamed of his nipples erect, pushed to my mouth, cock thrusting towards me, tassel discarded. A slickness oiled my fingers as I teased around my clit, head cramming my body with the thoughts of him hard inside me as I bit down. Him in me, cock and nipple. I juddered with orgasm, pressing again and again, but got up from the bed disappointed.

*

Work, so dull. Piles of paper, computers freezing. Only Alex kept me amused with his steady presence and gentle jokes. Such a shame, for me, that he was gay.

'I need supplies. Paper,' he said suddenly.

'I'll go if you want.' Alex had always used crutches and we'd exchanged a few experiences of dreaded 'special' school where, like him, I was sent as a kid with a chronic illness which I grew out of.

I sighed. Dave had used crutches too.

'Nah, thanks I'll be fine.'

As I typed drab rows of figures, the phone rang on Alex's desk. I leaned over and grabbed it dutifully.

'Alex, is that you?' A fast female voice said.

'He'll be back in a minute.' I was curious. 'Do you want to leave a message?'

There was a pause, the sound of slow breath, of thinking.

'Yes. I think I do. Tell him Sam rang. I am leaving. He's right. We've grown out of each other.'

'Oh, don't you think you should talk to him?' I gulped. Alex was very private, but I'd caught the name Sam. And made a very wrong conclusion.

'No. It's OK. We're past the angst stage.'

The phone clicked and she was gone.

The office didn't have a stationery cupboard but a strange small room which housed loads of general office supplies. It had a heavy door and a dingy light.

I went in and the door swung shut. I shivered at how cold it felt, a little window letting in a breeze.

Alex was pushing himself up on one crutch, muscles firm, as he stretched to reach a box with his other hand.

I was transfixed.

As he tensed, his shirt was tight across his broad chest. Two taut points pressed against the fabric.

'Alex, Sam rang,' I was breathless and agog.

He turned to face me. His perfect nipples turned too.

‘Oh. Well, I can guess the rest.’ He wasn’t surprised and lifted another packet.

I stood very close to him. Before I knew it I had my fingers fighting open his shirt.

Alex let a box fall to the floor.

My lips were around the left nipple first.

‘Oh ... Annie, Annie,’ he groaned.

I licked hard and the nipple stirred in my mouth.

‘If only you knew… how much… I’ve wanted someone to do that…’ His voice trailed off.

Warm, happy and horny as hell, I kept licking.

And licking. And biting.

And sucking.

And licking more. And more.

Our first happy thunderous fuck took place in the next five minutes and our nipples remained hard for the whole day